Earth Outpost 6-9

Amelia Dax

Acknowledgements

To the best people ever, who encouraged me to attempt this story, despite it being 'out-there', both in space and away from my usual public persona.

Table of Contents

THE HOOYA

DAMIAN

All quiet on the Western Front.

I laughed every time I thought of the line as I gazed out at the universe. It was the title of a novel about World War One. While the subject of isolation was on point, direction here was... pointless. We were in space where there was no west, east, or really any direction at all. The sun and Earth were behind us as our outpost faced the great beyond.

In our situation, quiet was always a good thing. Our monitoring equipment hummed along efficiently, detecting no trace of unexpected visitors to our part of the universe.

Perhaps I should catch you up. I'm Damian. I'm one of two people assigned to this station, Earth Outpost 6-9. Yeah, I chuckled at that, too. We are part of a network of three-hundred and sixty outposts, spaced one degree apart, orbiting around the sun just past the main asteroid belt between Mars and Jupiter. Our mandate: to be an early warning system to help protect Earth and our fledgling settlements on Mars from intergalactic marauders.

So far, Earth's experience with alien life forms had been sixty-forty. Sixty percent friendly and forty percent not so much.

Most of the aliens we'd encountered so far were highly intelligent. They were explorers, mapping out the vastness of space. They came to learn about us and often offered tips on how to further advance our species and our technology.

The Rothrengal had been particularly helpful. We met them for the first time back in Roman times, and more frequently in recent years, as our civilization finally developed enough to have something in common with them.

Let's face it. Compared to most of the life forms we've encountered; humans are toddlers who barely knew how to walk. We appreciate those willing to help our race survive to maturity.

There have been other visitors. Pirates, if you will. Species who came to rape and pillage our land, resources and people. Apparently, in some space cultures, we are a delicious afternoon snack.

Yeah, gave me the shivers too.

That's why the work Elin and I do is so important. Outposts like ours serve as the first contact for approaching ships. Our jobs are to identify already known friends and foes and introduce ourselves to new aliens who ventured into our solar system for the first time.

The computers did most of the work. We were just on location to provide the human touch when the cold logic of Artificial Intelligence just wasn't enough. Needless to say, we had a lot of downtime.

It was why I knew so much about history. I had hours to read. Our virtual library had every volume known to man and several translations of alien text to help us learn about the others who share the universe with us. But even with all that at my fingertips, it was a lonely existence.

Humans have always been social creatures. We are not good at being alone, which is why they assigned pairs to each outpost. They did rigorous testing for knowledge, skill, and personality to create partnerships that could survive the isolation of space without risk of us killing each other.

My counterpart, Elin, has been the perfect match for me in every way.

My specialties are history, language, and combat. Her strengths include culture and space geography. She is also an Empath, which would help if we ever met a species without verbal communication.

She was resting right now.

We have opposite sleep-wake schedules which allow us eight hours of rest and four hours together in between.

My favourite thing about her was she loved to play.

Often, I'd crawl into her bunk behind her and wake her by sliding in and out of her tight pussy while I toyed with her clit.

What can I say? Some outpost partners challenged each other with board games. Elin and I played with each other.

Usually, I was the more adventurous of the two of us, but lately she's been translating Rothrengal texts and has come across what seems to be their version of the Kama Sutra. Even though their body parts were distinctly different... I've woken up in the middle of Elin using new techniques that make me cum hard enough to dehydrate myself and still been erect and ready for the next round.

The Rothrengal are insatiable, and I loved them for it.

Alarms interrupt my reverie. The system detected something coming our way. The tenor of the sound let me know it was a friendly yet unscheduled vessel.

I jumped up from my lounger and raced to the monitors. No visual yet. It was still too far away and still had time to veer off in a different direction, never to be identified.

We got a lot of those, too. Galactic looky-loos.

But no, this one was heading straight for Earth, with our little outpost directly in its path.

The automatic hailing frequencies started chittering in every known language and signal type. It impressed me every time it engaged. We used everything from flashing lights, in spectrums not seen on Earth, to pulsates taught by those horny Rothrengal and those other friendly visitors to Earth who'd been willing to help the fledgling human species.

I turned off the audible alarms. Whatever it was it altered its trajectory slightly to bring it close to us but no longer on a collision course.

Elin appeared at my side, still wiping sleep from her eyes. She hadn't bothered to put on clothes and well, truth be told, I was naked too. Doing laundry is a bitch in space, so we only dressed for full-image calls with Earth Officials.

Even with the approaching danger, I rose to half mast, saluting her presence.

"What's coming?" Her body may have still been waking, but her brain was alert and processing the information she saw on the displays.

"Unknown. Scans show corporeal, humanoid-ish life-forms. About a dozen onboard."

"Match to the Alien Database of the Unmet." she ordered the system, as the computers buzzed with activity. "Oh." Her hand flew to her chest. "OH."

"What is it?" I asked, peering over her shoulder to see the screen and grinned. "Oh."

Her eyes lit with joy. "We get to meet them first." She clapped her hands. "They're coming right for us."

According to the information on the screen, these were the Hooya.

Beings so advanced, even the sexually focused Rothrengal viewed them as gods. Worth noting: their gods weren't pious and restrictive like most of the ancestral Earth religions. The information we had about the Hooya said they chased pleasure in all its forms.

My half-mast rose to fully loaded. We were about to get lucky. So, very, very lucky.

We watched as the speck on our monitor grew in size. Data flashed over multiple screens, heralding their approach. There was no doubt. Our little outpost in the middle of nowhere was indeed their destination.

"Should we get dressed?" Elin asked with a wicked twinkle in her eye.

"It is protocol." I responded. "Command will observe us if they come onboard."

"I'm sure those lame ducks back on Earth are used to seeing my delightfully perky ass."

"Yeah, but this will be global. Not just the jerk-offs who monitor us."

"Ah, true. We should attempt to make a proper first impression. Even if it's just to save ourselves from a lecture afterward." She flounced her very perky ass back to her sleeping quarters to change into her dress uniform.

I waited until she returned to the main area. She looked fresh and relaxed. You would never know she'd just been rudely awoken in the middle of her sleep cycle. Her eyes shone with anticipation. "Hurry, go get ready."

Once she settled in front of the displays, I sauntered in the opposite direction to make myself presentable. Although, if everything we've heard about this species was true, our efforts to clothe ourselves were in vain.

An hour later, earth standard time, the oddly shaped vessel drew up to our landing dock. It looked like a trident. Its tines were long and round, like many ships we'd seen, but theirs had oddly shaped ridges around the fuselage.

Elin and I both snickered. We'd seen the old commercials.

"Ribbed for her pleasure." She giggled.

"That can't be it." I said, trying to be logical.

"But is it wrong of me to hope so?" she quirked one eyebrow at me.

Thanks to the Rothrengal, our databases were already uploaded with a translator for the Hooyan language. They knew we would eventually come into contact with them.

The artificial intelligence in our outpost had already aided their ship to land. Well, perch really, on the edge of our loading dock. Their ship was easily five times the length of our station. The elevator tube had already attached itself to their entryway, and the pressure stabilized to where they could safely exit their ship and enter our facility.

The information the Rothrengal provided said they were larger than humans, with the same general shape. They warned us not to freak out because they also had two heads that moved independently yet spoke in stereo.

Elin and I stepped over to the greeting area, aware every camera in the vicinity was trained on the doors from the elevator tube. She grabbed my hand as we waited. "I am so wet right now," she said. "You could fuck me into next week and I'd still be soaked."

6

"And you haven't even seen them yet." I murmured. "I hope the Rothrengals weren't pulling our leg about them."

"Nope," she shook her head. "Not a chance. I've translated the texts. It's difficult for them to procreate, so they devote nearly all their time to finding ways to make sure their species survives."

Just then, the doors opened, and the advance committee of two Hooyas stepped forward. They were stunning. Their skin glowed with a purple radiance. Taller than me. They each stood over two meters. They were wide, shoulders spanning nearly the entire width of the doorway. Their heads adorned with hair-like tendrils caught up in complicated arrangements, adorned with shiny objects that shimmered.

They wore no garments.

The female came to us first. Her breasts were heavy and full... all four of them. Each was tipped with thick thumb-sized nipples. When she stood in front of us, she tilted her heads to the side in question. Her voice was melodious, speaking in a language I'd never heard.

"Why covered?" The AI translated.

"It's our tradition." Elin responded softly. Her voice filled with wonder.

The male stepped up beside the female. "You were bare before." His voice was accusatory.

Without meaning to, I glanced down at his genitalia. Not only had their ship looked like a phallic shape, but it was also, in fact, a replica of his penis. He was long and erect, with identical ridges. Except in person, the two smaller appendages moved fluidly around his stiff member.

"When it's us alone, we are." I said, meeting his gaze. "Our superiors feel it's proper to meet for the first time with clothes. We can remove them if you'd prefer." I tried to keep the eagerness out of my voice.

It was weird hearing the AI translate, speaking in a voice that sounded like me.

Our guests smiled at each other. "Yes." They spoke in unison, which, because of their two heads, sounded like their voices were coming at us from all corners of the room.

Elin and I must've looked like little kids being told they had unlimited time with Santa, as we stripped off the offending garments and tossed them aside.

As I bent down to remove my pants, I realized the woman Hooya also had the flowing appendages. One was on each side of her slit. They looked soft, and they seemed to stroke her as she watched me disrobe with interest.

Not that it was a contest, but it relieved me to see I was thicker than the Hooya male, I'm sure my eyes widened when I realized he didn't seem to have testicles. I immediately felt sorry for him. There was nothing like the feeling of your balls slapping against the ass of a woman while you're fucking her senseless.

Now that Elin and I were naked, our visitors looked us over. They chatted back and forth as they walked around us. The AI could not hear all they said because they were conversing so quietly. Secondary microphones would analyze their words later. In this moment, we had only their demeanor to assure us we weren't in danger.

They looked curious. The female said something to Elin, and the translator repeated, "May I?"

Elin nodded.

The female touched her breasts. Fondling them with a curious gentleness as she tested their weight in the palms of her alien hands.

"May I?" Elin asked before placing her own hands on the outer breasts of the Hooya woman. "They feel like mine," she whispered to me. "Only harder, like they're filled with water rather than flesh."

The male spoke. "They house our fertilizer."

Elin and I looked at each other in confusion then back at who we thought was the female. "So, you are the male? The propagator?"

"Yes." replied the female. Well, male, I guess, since she was the one with the testicles, despite them being shaped like boobs. "Copulation requires an external vessel to house the fertilizer for the suctioning, which mixes it with our seed. The vessel must be alive, and those you call Rothrengals told us of your existence and procreation process."

Elin's eyes got wide. "So, you need to fuck me with your boobs and then he has to suck the sperm out of me with his dick?"

"Elin!?" I whisper screamed to her. "Decorum. We're being watched."

Our visitors laughed. Their melodious words translated, "Do not worry. Your monitoring equipment's transmission has been… delayed." They stepped toward both of us but spoke to Elin. "We would very much like to attempt a procreation with you as our vessel."

Then the female… male, umm the one with breasts, turned to me. "I need to be stimulated to release the fertilizer." They reached out to fondle my still hard dick. "This intrigues me, as do these." They caressed my balls between the fingers of her other hand, and I nearly came on the spot.

"Come." Elin reached out to the other's hand. "I have an idea."

She led us down the hall to the guest sleeping quarters. In one of the spare bunkrooms for visiting crew, there was a family room. Bunk beds were along one wall, but the bottom bunk pulled out to be a larger bed able to accommodate two adults. Elin turned to face us once she extended the lower bed.

"From what I've read from Rothrengal scripts, this should work." She pointed at me. "Damian, lie down on your back across the bed, with your head toward the wall and your legs bent, feet on the floor."

Curious, I did as instructed.

"Ma'am" Elin pointed at the breasted alien.

"My name is Ina."

Elin smiled. "Ina, please straddle Damian and face the top bunk." Without questioning the plan, the alien towered above me as they put their knees outside of my thighs and sat lightly on my lap. The appendages between her legs moved excitedly. I just hoped Elin knew what she was doing. Those things looked strong enough to rip my cock from my body.

"Wait here." She said to the male, err female. Aw hell, the one with the dick.

"Ido," the alien pointed to himself. "I am Ido."

"Okay, Ido, please stand here. If I understand correctly, you won't be needed until later."

Ido nodded and stood where instructed.

Then Elin climbed up to the top bunk, hung her legs over the side and I heard a thump as her head hit the wall as she inched her way across the bunk far enough that her ass was at the edge.

Ina, reached up and placed Elin's legs on their shoulders, pulling Elin further off the bed but in a better

10

position to be fucked by those glorious tits. Then Ina raised themself from my body and inched forward.

I stroked myself a couple of times to smooth the pre-cum over the head of my cock. I remembered they said I was big. I didn't want to hurt them. Ready, I positioned my dick at their entrance and let them sink down on top of me. Fuck, they were tight. I could feel their inner muscles spasm as they tried to relax around my girth.

The AI couldn't translate the guttural melody, Ina exclaimed, as I pushed the rest of the way inside them.

Truthfully, no translation necessary.

Ido stood close, gripping their own dick and mimicked my motions, stroking from root to tip as I went in and out. They grabbed the top of the bunk to steady their legs.

Yeah buddy, I know.

Once Ina seemed comfortable, I topped them from the bottom. Pushing into them with a steady rhythm. It didn't take long until we moved in sync, and soon, we were all moaning in ecstasy.

I felt the appendages I'd been worried about sliding around to stroke my balls.

At first, they were petal soft as they licked and flicked at my tender flesh. Then, as the force of fucking increased, one teased at my asshole and the other gripped the base of my dick like a cock-ring. Trapping my hard on. Preventing my release.

I should have panicked, but it felt fucking incredible. I opened my eyes to see what was happening above me.

Elin was still spread-eagled on the top bunk.

Ina had one of their heads between Elin's legs, eating her out as if their life depended on it. Their other head was thrown back, mimicking Elin's cries of ecstasy.

Ina adjusted their arms so they could pull at the nipples of all four of their breasts in a quick, rhythmic pattern. Their nipples turned a deeper purple and shone with lubrication. They'd swollen to resemble short, thick cocks as Ina's hand pulled and tugged at them while still fucking the hell out of me and making Elin pant in ecstasy with one of their mouths.

Ido stood by, slowly stroking their genitals as they watched the show. Briefly I wondered what part they would play, but then Ina's wily tentacle twisted at my asshole, nearly making me explode with the need to cum.

Just as my eyes were about to roll back into my head, I heard Elin scream. My eyes flew open in time to see the alien above me fuck Elin with each of their long nipples. They swung their enormous tits in a blur as they pummeled Elin's pussy.

Long ropes of cum dripped toward me, but Ido leaned forward with their pelvis and immediately sucked them up with their dick.

It was something to see. The pronounced ridges I'd noticed earlier along his length rippled back and forth, creating a powerful suction that pulled the drops of semen out of the air before they landed on my torso.

Ina's tendrils released their grip on my cock.

I saw stars as wave after wave of orgasm hit me. I'd barely finished when she leaped off me in an obviously well practiced maneuver, and was replaced immediately by Ido, who stood on the lower bunk and started fucking Elin.

Ido didn't straddle me as their partner had done. They stood to the side and when it was apparent I was recovering, they nudged me hard enough to get me out of the way.

Elin hollered again. I wasn't sure if it was from pleasure or pain.

I rushed to my feet to see her thrashing about on the bunk as Ido's penis made the same sucking motions. Only this time, they was buried deep in my girl's cunt.

His long tendrils were busy, too. The one farthest from me had flattened and was circling Elin's clit like a tongue. The other one wound under Elin, probably prodding at her ass like Ina's had mine. Ido's hands caressed her breasts and tugged at her nipples, harder than I would have done.

Elin screamed again.

"He's going to hurt her." I said, as I reached out to stop the towering alien.

"She'll be fine." This time, Ina spoke directly to me instead of through the AI translator. "Ido is what you'd call, 'edging 'her until they can get all of my..." she paused while searching for the word the AI had used earlier. Finally, she said something in her language and the translator said. "Fertilizer."

Elin continued to grip the bedding on the bunk as the alien's penis continued to extend and withdraw. It was surreal to watch because their body didn't move, but their cock was going wild. Gyrating and plunging, while its tendrils moved in rhythm, driving Elin crazy with lust.

Ina took in a sharp breath. their high-pitched trill of excitement filled the room as the base of her partner's dick started glowing.

A few more strokes made Elin shatter with an intense orgasm. She went limp. Her ass and legs hanging off the bed without support, which caused her to almost topple to the lower bunk. Ido caught her just as she was starting to slide from the top mattress.

I reached her a split second later, and Ido carefully placed her in my arms.

"Holy fuck, Damian." she said weakly. "That was fucking amazing."

I was still weak in the knees myself. "Baby, can you stand?"

"Sure." She nodded. "I think so."

As soon as I put her feet on the ground, I held her close. At this point, we were so spent, I wasn't sure which of us was holding the other one up.

Both of the Hooya bowed deeply before us. "We are forever grateful to you. We have successfully procreated.

Ina gestured toward the purple hued glow that spread from Ido's cock to their midsection. "Our bodies have become toxic to our fertilizer, which poisons our seed. We've exhausted artificial methods. Our bodies continue to evolve in a way that will eventually cause our extinction. We've been searching for new hosts to aid in our mating process."

"You mean Elin's pregnant?" I didn't care that they were almost half a meter taller than me. "You don't just randomly knock up the puny human."

"No, No." Ina said. "I put our fertilizer in her, and then Ido, who in your Earth terms is my wife, sucked it out to fertilize our seed. They are glowing, which means it worked. We shall have offspring."

Elin looked like she finally understood. "I've been reading your translations and didn't understand that you require four to mate. Now, it all makes sense." She whispered to me. "I thought they were just kinky."

"When the Rothrengals encountered your species, they contacted us and suggested human females may be compatible hosts for the fertilizer and the males might be similar enough in physical dimensions to be able to initiate the fertilization process."

Ido spoke up. "We will be forever thankful to both you and to the Rothrengals. I despaired of ever conceiving."

"I'm glad we could help." Elin spoke. Despite her exhaustion, I could see the awe in her face as we realized what we'd just done.

"Anytime." I offered.

"We were hoping you would say this." Their voices echoing around us in stereo again as we walked back out into the main room.

Ina and Ido walked clasped together, close enough for their heads to intertwine.

Elin and I walked at a slower pace. I'm sure her legs felt like wet noodles as much as mine.

Apparently, it wasn't just the monitor's signal to Earth, they delayed. They took our security system offline too.

As our guests entered our greeting area, there was a collective gasp.

The rest of the occupants from their ship stood in our control room, marveling at Ido's glowing midsection.

For an instant I felt fear, understanding how vulnerable we were. The rest of the occupants of their ship had boarded our outpost, without us knowing.

The crowd grew excited as they reverently touched Ido's glowing middle. Then there was a slight surge toward us. As if each pair were eager to be next.

Elin smiled up at me. Anticipation already overriding her fatigue. "I think we're going to need coffee. Lots of coffee."

GHOST GNOME

ELIN

It was a long night at the outpost.

Damian was on his sleep-cycle, and I was bored and horny. Then again, when wasn't I horny?

They'd done a great job of matching personalities when they paired us together on Earth Outpost 6-9. I don't think it was a coincidence they assigned us to this particular post because the name suited us a little too well.

Damian was as insatiable as I was and twice as adventurous. Which wasn't a bad thing, trust me.

When you're stationed in the middle of nowhere, staring out into the endless vastness of space, 'missionary' could only hold your interest for so long.

Most of our visitors were of the same mindset. Damian and I have already had a few adventures while welcoming our very friendly space-neighbours.

The Hooya have become regular visitors since they learned humans are a safe and effective addition to their mating process. In fact, there is a whole new division at the Space Exploration Center on Earth to help facilitate their pregnancies.

But since Damian and I were the first, Ina and Ido, our Hooyan friends, stop by with their children every time they're in our part of the universe. It was always a fun time after their kids went to sleep.

Just thinking about the orgasms I've had courtesy of the Hooya had me trailing my hand between my legs. Neither Damian nor I bothered with clothes when we were alone. Sure, we were monitored by a crew on Earth, but after the initial protests claiming our nakedness wasn't professional, no one kicked up a fuss.

Honestly, I'm sure they've enjoyed watching us cavort about without clothing. In fact, I've heard rumours of an unusually long waiting list to be considered for our monitoring team.

I shifted on the chair, and threw one leg up over the arm, spreading my legs open so the breeze from the air distributor could blow directly on my clit as I fingered myself. I let my head fall back and played as I watched the universe float by on the ceiling monitors.

I'd just about lulled myself to sleep when I felt more than just my fingers playing with my pussy. "Damian." I said sleepily. "You're not supposed to be awake yet."

He didn't respond and seriously, he was a big boy. If he didn't want a proper sleep, he could deal with the consequences. I was going to lie back and enjoy his efforts.

I moved my hands up my body and started tugging gently at my nipples while Damian kept up his exploration of my nether regions. He nudged my legs wider, and I spread them as far as I could. The pleasant sensations were light and soothing as I drifted back into my state of bliss. I didn't feel him move, yet his cock nudged at my entrance. Always up for a fuck, I reached down to spread the lips of my cunt, inviting him in.

I smiled as my fingers grazed his cock. He must have been playing in the lab again. Damian was always creating condoms that mimicked alien skin textures. Some did amazing things to my inner walls as they stimulated nerve endings in ways a smooth human penis just couldn't do.

What made it better was that it was Damian who was fucking me. Not just a lifeless piece of silicone.

I reached down to give him a stroke before he entered me and to feel the texture he'd created this time.

The surface felt harder than usual. The sheath wasn't as thin as Damian usually preferred. He found that when the material was too thick, it lessened the sensation for him. Unless... maybe he did something with the inside for a little self-stimulation.

This version had bumps with small clumps of hair that felt slightly stiff to my touch. It concerned me until I felt them bend beneath my fingers. Whew, they wouldn't scratch.

Still without opening my eyes, I guided him inside.

His first thrust was tentative, as if not sure how far he could go.

I thought that odd, but maybe he'd done something to the tip to extend his length. That could be fun.

His next thrust was more certain.

Then three things happen simultaneously:

He filled me with his cock, and started sucking and flicking my tender clit with his tongue.

The station's alarms screeched.

And Damian screamed, "What the Fuck." from across the room.

My eyes flew open. How could he be over there when he was balls deep in me?

My head snapped up just in time to see the ugliest little troll with his lips still on my clit as his chin slid out of my cunt, shiny with my arousal.

He winked and waved at me before disappearing into thin air.

Damian bolted toward the monitors.

I followed at a slower pace as I tried to absorb what I'd just seen. It was real. I had the pussy juices streaming down my inner thighs to prove it. It was also surprising to me I was more upset about being interrupted than about what had been fucking me.

The computers whirred as they tried to identify the intruder.

I'd sensed no ill intent, which was partially why I'd assumed my fucker was Damian. "At least he seemed friendly." I joked.

Damian looked angrier than I'd ever seen him. "It's not funny, Elin. No one has the right to fuck you without your permission."

"I thought it was you." I shrugged. "Hell, I held my held myself open for him."

"Yeah, but you thought it was me. That makes a difference."

"Damian, I don't know why you're so upset. It's not like I haven't fucked aliens before."

"Yeah, but we don't know what that guy was doing to you. We don't even know who or what he was."

I thought back to the gentle way the creature had touched me in exploration. "He wasn't trying to harm me."

"Just because he looked like one of Snow White's seven dwarfs doesn't mean he's harmless."

"Well, he's probably grumpy now because he didn't get to finish." I know I was definitely not happy. Whatever he was, he was fantastic.

"Oh, for fuck's sake, Elin. This is not funny."

"Come on, Damian. It is just a little funny. I mean, if you ignore the whole 'How the hell did he get in here? 'part."

I paused, "And how come it wasn't until he was fucking me with his chin that the sensors went off? How did he avoid them until then?"

As I worked at the systems, trying to identify our visitor, I felt a tickle along the inside of my ankle. I looked down to see my little friend, barely visible, nuzzling my calf as his long tongue teased and licked the juices that ran down my leg. Just the sight of it made me fantasize about the things it could do to me.

Then I realized he was semi-transparent. His touch was very light, similar to when he first touched me. That's when it dawned on me. He hadn't been hesitant after all. The sensors hadn't seen him because he hadn't been completely corporeal. It was only when he became solid enough to thrust his long chin into my channel that the alarms went off.

With that thought came another. How long had he been in our outpost watching us?

Had he been observing the different ways we've had sex? The different species we've had sex with. Listening in on our conversations about who we'd like to meet and what positions we'd like to try when we had sex with them? He definitely seemed to understand our language.

I knew I should let Damian know the alien was caressing my inner thigh and inching his way back toward my cunt. Instead, I widened my stance to give him better access. I wanted to see what he could do with that tongue of his.

This little fellow knew exactly what he was doing. It took only minutes, and I was in danger of having a very loud orgasm.

During his ministrations he'd come around in front of me, poised to insert that humongous chin of his back into my pussy despite Damian standing beside me. I pretended to drop something and squatted until I was face to face with my new little friend.

I mouthed the words, "My bedroom, now." I stood back up and said to Damian. "I need to go to the bathroom and clean up. I'll be back in a few minutes."

"That's a good idea." he said. "Take a shower and wash yourself well. We don't know what kind of disease that thing may accidentally have given you."

"Yeah, will do." I smiled to myself as I walked away. "Damian just gave me extra playtime."

Silently, my little companion trotted along beside me. He stayed semi-transparent, thus undetectable by the ship's monitors.

Once we were in my quarters, I said," You have to stay like this. If you become solid, the ship will know you're here and alert Damian."

My new friend nodded his head. Then the cheeky monkey pointed at me and then put his finger up to his lips in the universal sign to be quiet and winked at me. Apparently, he had been around long enough to observe how loud I can get.

I nodded and reached over to turn on the shower to help mask any noise. I leaned against the vanity, and I spread my legs, offering a silent invitation for him to continue where he left off.

Part of me I thought I was nuts.

Even semi-transparent, his skin was the sickliest shade of green. His chin was covered in hard lumps with grotesque looking hair growing out of them. I'm glad I had felt him before I saw him, otherwise I don't think I could have brought myself to have sex with him. But now, I knew the hair was soft, and the way it stimulated my inner walls was off the charts. And those bumps. Oh my God, even the few strokes I'd felt earlier were just enough of a teaser to let me know I was in for a treat.

His tongue curled out like a cartoon frog's. It was long and thick. He flattened it at the end as it stroked my clit.

I had to bite my hand not to moan out loud.

Then he moved forward and used his short, stubby fingers to make sure I was wet. Not that he needed to worry. I'd been soaked since he first touched me.

Next, he slowly pushed his chin into me. It was a sight to see. It had just the slightest curve up at the end, which hit my g-spot as it slid past. Those bumps were exquisite.

I tightened around him, bringing me to an instant orgasm. My world turned into a white kaleidoscope as my body shuddered around him. It vaguely registered that his hands stabilized my legs so I wouldn't collapse.

He was far from done with me. As I came back to the present, he slowly moved his head back and forth, his lips sealed on to my clit again as he eased his chin in and out of me.

It was glorious.

My hands gripped either side of my small vanity and I opened my knees wider, giving him as much access as I could while still standing up. "I'm not going to be sorry for this, am I?" I whispered. "There's nothing in your physiology that will harm me?"

He shook his head slightly back and forth, which sent another wave of pleasure through me. Flickers of electricity tingled through my arms and all the way down to my toes.

His lips hummed against me as if he was trying to say something but couldn't because, well, you know, his mouth was full. It took him only four more strokes before I was shattering around him again. My channel convulsed around his chin. He lapped at my pussy, sucking up my honey. His long tongue lapped down under his chin to ensure he didn't miss a drop.

When he finished, he pulled his chin out from me.

I gave him a small towel to wipe my moisture from his face.

"Can you speak?" I asked him in a low voice.

He pointed to his body and shook his head.

"If you weren't transparent, could you?"

He nodded.

"You're not here to hurt us?"

He looked offended. He gestured down to his crotch and made a pulling motion as if he was jerking off.

"So, you're just here to fuck me?"

He nodded vigorously. Then he held up his finger for me to wait and took a step back from me and unclasped his pants. If I thought his chin was impressive, his cock was beyond belief. It was as thick as my forearm and at least 10 inches long. Like his chin, his cock was covered in bumps.

I could already imagine how they'd feel thrusting in and out of me.

"I have to get cleaned up and go back out before Damian comes looking for me. Will you be here later?"

God, I felt like I was cheating on my husband, but Damian had been so angry, I doubted he'd let me do hands on research the way I wanted. Sneaking around was my only option.

My new friend nodded yes and faded away into nothing. It was unnerving because I didn't know where he was. If this was what being haunted was like? I rubbed my thighs together. Sign me up.

I rushed to finish cleaning up so Damian wouldn't worry and come looking for me.

It surprised me how upset he was over my ghostly gnome. Maybe he was upset because he wasn't included in the fun. I mean, we've both had separate lovers before, depending on the species, but this was the first one that I had done independently, and who sought me out specifically when Damian wasn't around.

Another mystery to solve.

Back at the panel, Damian apologized. "I'm sorry for jumping all over you." he said. "When the alarms sounded and I came rushing out, it looked like you were dead. It scared me. I thought he hurt you."

"Ironically, I thought he was you." I smiled at him. "I thought you'd been experimenting with skin textures and for a fun surprise was fucking me with your newest creation." I teased. "For the record, it was fucking fantastic. I think that's why I was so surprised at your reaction, because it's nothing we haven't done before."

"But we've always agreed to the adventure. We always knew who we were playing with." Damian pointed out. "He took you with no type of screening. Who knows what sort of disease he gave you?"

"True, but he apologized." I recognized my mistake as soon as I spoke.

"What do you mean, 'He apologized'?"

"He and I had a little semitransparent pantomime while I was cleaning up. It seems our sensors only pick him up when he's fully visible."

"None of these fucking sensors we have on board can detect him when he's invisible?" Damian grew angry again.

"No, but it's okay. He comes in peace. He says the only thing he wants to do is have sex with me."

"Well, he already did that."

"Not exactly. That was just his chin. You should see his dick."

Despite his irritation, Damian looked intrigued. "Tell me."

"Hang on." I turned toward the controls. "Now that I've had a better look at him, let me see if I can find him. My hands moved across the keyboard, searching the database for a short gnome-like alien who could disappear into thin air. A few seconds later, a hologram of my new lover appeared."

"Holy crap." Damian said. "How do you even pronounce their name?"

"I'm just going to call him my little gnome."

He shrugged. "Okay, gnome it is."

Together, we scanned the displayed information from the knowledge base. The Rothrengal had given us basic information from every species they'd encountered. They had very little detail about our new little friend.

The most important thing to me was that he came from an allied species who enjoyed exploring new worlds and learning from other cultures. They weren't poisonous to humans, which had been one of Damian's fears.

They were a shy species and had developed the unique ability to remain invisible. In their transparent phase, they defied detection by less sophisticated surveillance systems, and according to the Rothrengal, ours was primitive.

"I guess we can remove him from the threat category." Damian admitted. "But I'd still like to be warned when he comes around."

"I suspect he'll let us know in a minute, since he's probably watching us right now."

As if on cue, my little gnome appeared behind us, followed a second later by the ship's warning system.

Damian quickly shut down the sound, and we both turned to greet our new friend.

"So, you're just here to fuck Elin?"

The gnome clapped his hands and nodded. Despite his gruff, grotesque appearance, his voice was high pitched and melodious. Like a small child singing a nursery rhyme. "Yes please. Very much please."

"Why did you sneak up on Elin? Why didn't you announce yourself?"

"I scared. You big. Me small."

Damian looked at me and shrugged. "I guess he's got a point."

"You won't inadvertently endanger me, will you?" I asked. Getting knocked up by an alien was not really part of my career path. I'm supposed to be artificially infertile while on the station, but even that's not one hundred percent guaranteed. Especially with alien sperm.

The gnome shook his head. "No. Me not hurt."

"And you can't make me pregnant?"

"No, we…" He paused. "We re-produce, split in two." He made an up and down slicing motion with his hand.

Damian nodded. The answer seemed to satisfy him as well. "Can I watch?" he asked.

I swear the little gnome's cheeks turned rosy. "Not normal." he said but held up his finger to halt Damian's next statement. "Me watch you. It equal."

Even though I'd cleaned up not 10 minutes earlier, I was already wet again. I didn't even notice I'd started rubbing my thighs together, but both men did.

"Where would you like this to happen?" I asked the gnome.

A smile spread across his face. He'd obviously already thought of this from the way he crooked his finger.

We followed him down the hall to the family unit. He barely looked at the larger bed and patted the mattress of the child's bed that was considerably lower to the ground. He pointed at me and said, "Elly, sit."

I smiled at his attempt to say my name.

His childish tone was in such contrast to the bulge in his pants. He nudged my knees apart as soon as my ass hit the mattress. His pants disappeared without him disrobing.

"That's handy." Damian said.

I reached out and stroked my hand along his thick, green penis. It surprised me how the tufts of hair growing out of these bumps were softer than on his chin. His girth equaled my wrist.

I looked over at Damian. "Can you see?"

He'd taken up residence on a small chair at the foot of the bed. He looked very intrigued. "May I touch it too?"

The little gnome nodded his head vigorously. "Touch feel good."

Together, Damian and I stroked and gently pulled our new little friend's cock. His balls were heavy, which made me curious, since they didn't reproduce sexually.

He must have read the confusion on my face.

He said. "From before we learned split."

"Are you ready?" I asked him. I knew I was.

"Please. Yes, please."

I leaned back on the bed and braced myself up on my elbows. I wanted to watch this. My body tingled in anticipation as Damian reached down and spread my lips for our friend.

The little guy stood forward and his cock slowly disappeared into my pussy.

I could feel myself stretch around him.

When he was halfway in, he pulled out slightly, and then pushed in again. Allowing my natural lubrication to smooth his way. He was like nothing I'd ever felt before.

My walls expanded and contracted around every bump on his dick. The short hairs added a soothing sensation with each controlled thrust.

Damian looked impressed as I took more and more of the gnome's hard, green cock inside me. "You're not going to feel me for a week after this." he joked. Despite his complaint, the sight still turned him on. He jerked himself off in sync with the gnome's pace.

It took a few minutes until I could finally take the gnome's cock all the way. I hadn't noticed earlier, but he had a little nub at the base of his penis. It wasn't hard enough to be bone, but from the way his eyes rolled back in his head when it collided with my pubis, it was an extra sensitive piece of anatomy. I braced myself on one elbow and reached forward to rub it as he thrust in and out of me.

"Oh good. Good." He panted as he pumped faster.

The three of us kept a steady rhythm. The gnome's cock in my cunt. Damian jerking off, and me stroking the gnome's little nub.

Our moans filled the room.

Damian was the first to let go. His load landed over the gnome's shoulder and back.

That was enough to set the gnome off. He plunged into me with short, quick strokes before he threw his head back and screamed something in his own language. The jerky movement of him cumming and ramming against my clit sent me into orbit. My walls clenched around his cock, which made his eyes open in surprise, before he threw his head back and howled again.

I collapsed back onto the bed. My arms were no longer able to support my weight.

The gnome fell forward, his head resting on my stomach.

Damian draped spread-eagled over his chair as if someone tossed him there. His hands dangling toward the floor. "Holy Shit, that was hot."

We lay like that until the station buzzed an alert. Playtime had ended. We had work to do. "I've got this. You clean up." Damian rose to his feet and left the room.

I sat up and leaned forward to give my gnome a hug, ignoring the dollop of Damian's spunk dripping down the gnome's back. "Thank you." I said to him, "That was unbelievable."

I swear he blushed again.

"Me help clean." He turned his head and flicked his tongue over his shoulder to clean Damian's mess. "Eww." White spittle flew over me. "No taste good." He took his finger and swabbed the fluid from my stretched channel. "Taste."

I bent down to lick his finger. Instead of the salty tang of a human male, he tasted sweet. "Much better." I nodded.

"You like him's?" He looked perplexed.

"Not really, but it's a small price to pay for the fun I have with him."

He thought for a moment and then nodded. "Make sense."

He bent again and used his tongue to clean my pussy. It wasn't arousing this time. His touch felt soothing on my inner walls as he licked. By the time he finished, I was half asleep.

I felt the mattress move beside me as he touched his forehead to mine. "Thank you, Elly."

I opened my eyes in time to see him fade from sight. "Wait. Will we see you again?"

He reappeared so he could speak. "Might. Need go now. Too long one place." He blew a kiss as he faded into nothing.

Damian returned to my bedroom. "Is he gone?"

"Yeah," disappointment clouded my voice. "He said he'd been here too long."

"That's too bad. He would have been fun to keep around."

"True. He even helped me clean up." Then I smirked as I looked at Damian's cock, hard with another drop of pre-cum, ready in case there was more action. "Oh, and by the way, he doesn't like the taste of your spunk either."

SPATIUM CIMEX

ELIN

Damian and I sat in our chairs at the bank of monitors and watched the Outpost 6-9 monitoring system. Our station, like its sister stations that surrounded Earth, was always on alert for visitors to our small corner of the universe.

Most of the surveillance turned up nothing, but occasionally we found the odd anomaly here and there that required a closer look. Today we were chasing an elusive reading that didn't seem to be a ship but was definitely more than random space debris.

Our servers churned as they tried to identify the small objects slowly approaching us, when suddenly, the mass that by all data points should be still thousands of kilometers away came into view.

Damian visibly paled. "Oh, no."

"What?" I asked frantically, searching to see how this was possible. Unless what we were looking at was separate from whatever our sensors were tracking.

"Space Bugs." He whispered.

The strangled tone of his voice made me whip around in my chair to look at him. In all the time we'd been stationed here together, I'd never seen him scared and right now he was terrified.

"We're dead." He said as he flopped into his seat and looked hopelessly at the window to watch the bugs' approach.

I followed his gaze as the flow of many tiny beings drew closer. I concentrated on their movement and tried to reach out to them. Part of the reason I'd been chosen for the Earth Outpost Program was that I was a Diamond Level Empath. My parents discovered my natural sensitivity early in my childhood and they encouraged me to develop it. As I grew up, I sought proper training to use it more effectively.

Despite Damian's dire prediction, I sensed only curiosity and caution. They seemed to have no ill intent toward us.

The outpost's monitoring system still didn't pick up their presence even though some of the first 'bugs', as Damian called them, landed on our window.

"I'm not going down without a fight." Damian jumped up and shouted defensive instructions to the station's control.

I whispered into my consol. "Override Sequence 563977QW1" which immediately brought all systems under my control. It was a safety measure put in place in case a member of outpost crew went bat-shit crazy. It happened, occasionally. The isolation and loneliness from being stuck in space made people a little bonkers.

Damian stopped short when he realized what I'd done. "What the fuck Elin?" He strode toward me. "We have to defend ourselves."

"Damian. Calm down." I spoke softly, trying to infuse him with my calm. "I feel no aggression from them."

"But they can destroy entire ships by eating through their hulls."

"Damian, baby, look at them." I took his hand and drew him close to the window. I opened my senses to the creatures outside the hull and felt a wave of gratitude from them. "They are curious. They mean us no harm." I said as I placed my hand against the reinforced glass. The bugs scurried out of the way until they realized I couldn't touch them. Then they edged back, like curious little puppies. Tracing the outline of my palm and chasing my fingers when I moved them.

"See."

"But there are lists of ships these creatures have destroyed." Damian argued.

"Perhaps it was in self-defense." I suggested. "Our station is a lot bigger than they are. Hell, they are tiny. I could probably fit three of them in the palm of my hand." I nodded back to the window where the creatures were taking turns playing with my fingers as I lightly moved them back and forth. "Look at them. They are content. Perhaps they were just looking for a place to rest."

They were fascinating. They looked like they were made of soft translucent jelly, and the way they moved reminded me of an octopus I'd seen at an aquarium as a child. Except these little fellows had no limbs to speak of, they just gracefully undulated across the outer surface of our ship. I couldn't see any features. No eyes, nose or mouth, just a circular mass spanning less than ten centimeters apiece.

"So, what do we do now?" Damian asked, obviously still pissed that I'd shut him out of the station's systems.

"We wait." I said as I walked back to where he'd slumped in his chair. "The tactile sensors still haven't picked them up. I doubt they're causing any damage." I glanced back at the monitors that were still tracking the other anomaly. Apparently, it had turned away and left our quadrant. "See, we're back to normal."

"Except I'm still locked out of the system and there are space bugs staring at me." He was pouting.

"Damian, they don't have eyes." I sighed as I leaned over and kissed him. "They can't stare at you." I reached down to stroke his cock.

As usual, neither of us wore clothes. Sure, they constantly monitored us from Earth, but no one complained anymore about our nudity. Between the two of us and our occasional extra-terrestrial encounters, there was something for everyone to watch, no matter their persuasion.

Damian was still freaking out. His cock remained flaccid in my hand, so I dropped to my knees and swallowed his length until I could kiss his balls. He didn't stay limp for long.

Damian shut his eyes and dropped his head back as arousal temporarily quieted his objections.

As I sucked and stroked Damian's cock, I sensed a growing interest from the creatures outside. Slowly, without Damian noticing, I turned the chair around and shifted my position to the side, giving our new friends a view of what I was doing. I licked up the length of his cock and then closed my lips over the tip, sucking gently as I playfully tugged at his balls and lazily circled his anus with my finger.

Soon, he began to thrust into my mouth.

I took him all the way to the back of my throat, and I played with his balls. When I felt them tighten, I released him from my mouth and jerked him off, watching his cum shoot across his abs and chest.

Our little buddies practically vibrated against the glass of our window in excitement as Damian sighed in contentment. "Okay, I promise I won't try to clean the bugs off the windshield."

"Good, because I think they really enjoyed watching you shoot your load." The look of horror on his face made me laugh. "Damian, we've had sex with every alien race we've encountered. Why is this any different?"

"They're bugs."

"They're cute." I shot back at him and then I wandered back over to watch them flow back and forth over our viewing window, still undetected by our station's external sensors.

These little guys were just hanging out. It made me more certain that they'd attacked those other ships out of self-defense. Damian's first instinct had been to attack. I wonder if the other ships attempted to harm this swarm, colony, or whatever you wanted to call it.

The size of the cluster of them coming toward our outpost had been impressive. I'd bet, if they spread out, they could cover most of our station.

Curious, I flipped on the external cameras while trying to ease their collective minds. I meant no harm.

I felt a rush of apprehension, but then a soothing vibration. They understood I wanted to watch them as they'd watched us. Like chameleons back on Earth, they blended in with our station. They would be invisible to any approaching craft until it came close enough to dock.

Amazing.

Damian stood behind me, his attention bouncing between the window and the display screen for the cameras. "We are so screwed if they get mad."

"Then don't make them mad." I stated the obvious. "They enjoyed watching me go down on you. Should we show them how we have sex?"

"You don't find them creepy?"

"It's not like there will be thousands of eyes staring at us. They're sensory rather than visual." I laughed at him.

"You won't even know they're there. Plus, the more relaxed you are, the more relaxed they will be."

"So, you're telling me we should have sex to ensure our safety?"

"Yeah, something like that." I winked and dropped the armrests on the chair he'd been sitting in earlier, to give me room to straddle him. "You don't even have to see them." I told him as I turned the chair around to face the doorway leading to the other parts of the station instead of the monitors and window.

When I looked back at Damian, he was already hard and heading my way.

He sat on the chair facing away from our observers and I put my foot on the lowered armrest in a not-so-station-appropriate-use action and then mounted his lap like a horse. I didn't immediately slide down his pole. I spread my legs wide and ran my pussy lips over his hard cock until he was as wet as I was. I closed my eyes and enjoyed the feel of him gliding through my folds.

The flutter of excitement that shot through our audience made me almost cum on the spot. Their reactions grew stronger until they felt like a physical touch.

The sensation was so strong, I opened my eyes to see a steady stream of the little creatures sliding into the room with us. I glanced over at the monitors, and they were silent. It was still as if these little space creatures didn't exist. There was no indication of a hull breach, yet they flowed into the room through the multiple layers of specialized glass like a waterfall.

They ebbed and flowed over my feet and up my legs as if awaiting my reaction.

I resisted my instinctive urge to kick them away.

Their intent hadn't changed. Through our empathic connection, I feel soothing vibrations and growing feelings that increased the sensations I felt as Damian's hard cock rubbed against me.

I looked at Damian and noticed the bugs were careful not to touch him. I could only assume they could sense his hesitation and fear about their arrival and didn't want to incite his wrath or do anything to endanger their existence.

They didn't communicate with words or even images. They seemed to be a type of hive-mind, entirely dependent on feelings and sensations to communicate. Fear, excitement, arousal.

Yeah, these little guys understood arousal.

I held out my hand to where they patiently waited for me to decide what to do. As soon as I put my hand toward the closest one, it flowed its body onto my fingers and up my arm.

They followed, one after the other, until my entire body was covered with their pulsating presence. They amplified every movement as I slid against Damian. Not just those physically against my skin, but I could feel the instant echo as the sensations traveled in wave after wave to the tiny beings still outside our outpost and back again.

It was an incredible sensation, and I wanted more.

I rose above Damian, taking his cock in my hand and stroking him up and down, spreading his pre-cum over the head. I teased my opening with his mushroom shaped glans before I pushed myself down over him until our bodies met. Then I ground my clit against him, enjoying the intensity of pleasure from the friction.

The wave of sensation enveloped me from a thousand angles as it transmitted through the mass. I moved again, needing the feeling of Damian inside me to balance the external sensations.

Our visitors moved with me. Their arousal was palpable as they shared the pleasure I experienced with every stroke of his cock against my inner walls.

I tightened my muscles to give Damian's cock a squeeze and I could almost hear their silent tittering. Then I felt the sensation of being lifted. I looked down to realize they were separating Damian and me while flowing into the gaps left behind. As they carried me away, they recreated the shape and feel of my body over Damian.

Unaware of the change, Damian continued to fuck them with the same intensity as he'd been nailing me.

My cunt was still full. I looked down to see they'd formed a replica of Damian and were moving in and out of me as he had been doing a few seconds ago. I clenched around them and rotated my hips.

As expected, the reaction to my movement spread throughout their collective.

They enveloped me with warmth and sensual touching over every inch of my skin, as if a million mouths were sucking and licking.

I spread my pussy lips open to give them access to my clit. As soon as they touched the sensitive nerve endings, I exploded around them. My orgasm ricocheted through the mass, coming back to me in waves that started another climax. A never-ending orgasm.

I heard Damian gasp and I looked over at my partner.

He was also suspended in a sea of our new friends as they flowed around him. "Holy Fuck." He said when our eyes met. "Fuck, this is insane. I've never cum this hard in my life." He gasped and then closed his eyes.

To my utter shock, Damian laid his head back on the pillow of undulating space bugs and gave himself over to the pleasure.

I felt his surrender through the mass, along with my own pleasure, which they reflected back at me. I felt the tension as his balls tightened as if they were my own and felt his release as I watched him cum again, spraying over the backs of the tiny creatures surrounding us.

The sensations echoed along my channel as if he'd just blown his load inside me. My muscles tightened again, and I ground myself against the creatures. They seemed to sense what I needed. They thickened and pushed against my clit, which set me off again.

Instead of feeling exhausted after multiple orgasms, I felt energized. Could someone die from pleasure?

"I don't care." Damian answered aloud, "They can destroy me from the inside out if this is what it feels like."

"Oh God, yes." I agreed as pleasure flooded my senses again.

Minutes, hours. It could have been days or weeks, for all I knew. We lost all sense of time and place. We became part of their energy cycle. I heard beeps, buzzes and even flashing lights in the background, but my senses had prioritized pleasure over everything else.

Damian and I were lost in the haze of euphoria.

Then we weren't.

The little space bugs parted like the red sea to lay us on the floor. They still radiated joy, but there was now an undertone of caution and concern. Some still covered us in a layer of what I could only perceive as protection, but the feelings of arousal and intense pleasure had dissipated.

It left me feeling bereft as I slowly regained awareness of my surroundings. It was as if I was coming back into myself after an out-of-body experience.

Damian had managed to sit up. His appearance startled me. His cheeks were hollow and gaunt, accented by heavy dark circles under his eyes. Then I realized the station's warning systems were going haywire. Not because of the space bugs, or an approaching attack, but because our physical conditions had deteriorated. Our wellness monitors screeched. On the main monitors, I could see our control team on Earth. They were frantically calling our names and peering at their screens so closely that I saw more nostrils than I could count.

"They've reappeared." Someone shouted to the room back on Earth. "I see Damian, and Elin's head just surfaced. They're okay."

I lifted my hand to wave, and it shocked me at how heavy and foreign it felt. When I looked at it, my skin was translucent and loose over my knuckles and tendons.

"Are you guys all right?"

Damian grabbed the arm of the chair I'd lowered to the floor and pulled himself to his knees. The creatures flowed around him as if offering their support as he maneuvered himself onto the chair. "How long were we out?" His voice was scratchy and hoarse.

"We lost sight of you three days ago. We could still read your vitals, so we didn't worry too much until they started declining over the past few hours."

"Three days?" I asked from my spot on the floor. "No wonder I'm ravenous and feel like I could drink the station dry.

"We have Edward and Stacey on their way to you."

41

Damian and I looked at each other in horror.

"Can you recall them?" Damian asked.

Edward, never Ed, and Stacey were the staunchest of rule followers and made no secret of their distaste for the type of space exploration Damian and I excelled at.

Several smirks were visible in the control room back on Earth. "Sorry. They were the closest. You're sure you don't need a hand for a few days while you recover?"

"We'll be fine." I assured Control. "We were never in any danger. There was just a misjudgment of the limits of our physiology."

"So, how did you disappear?"

"You can't see them?" Damian asked, surprised.

"Station: lower lights." I said, and the overhead lights dimmed, leaving only the illumination from the computer system.

"Holy Shit."

"What are they?" Voices rang out from the speakers.

I stood rather shakily and, with help from my little friends acting as an exoskeleton to ensure I didn't fall, I pulled up the information file we had on the space bugs. Spatium Cimex Mortis, Space Death Bugs. "We're going to have to update our information on these little fellows. They're an empathic species. They are curious but harmless as long as they sense no danger to themselves."

"How'd they get in? We showed no sign of entry?"

"They came through the ship. None of our sensors picked them up. But I watched them seep through the hull without doing damage. It's as if they dissolved and reformed once inside."

"But they destroyed all those other ships?"

"I suspect our little friends acted in self-defense after the other ships tried to exterminate them." I shrugged. "Damian's first instinct was to protect our station as well, even though I sensed no ill intent from them and then felt their relief when we didn't try to kill them." I stroked my hand over the mass as it stayed close as I spoke. "They are very friendly."

"Friendly?" Damian chuckled. "That's one word for it." He stood and walked over to the small unit beside the bank of monitors and pushed a few buttons, but nothing happened. "Elin? Can I have access again?"

"Cancel Override Sequence 563977QW1." I told the computer.

Damian pressed the buttons again and this time, a click and two whirs sounded before he returned, carrying two open containers of green-grey liquid. It was a nutrition-blast smoothie, which looked disgusting, but it tasted sweet, like apples. "Drink this. We're both severely dehydrated."

When I took a sip, I could feel the collective gasp of our friends as they tracked the path if the soothing cool beverage as it passed over my parched throat.

In seconds, they'd flowed into a human form beside me.

I passed my drink to it. "Be careful. Just take a small sip."

The form nodded and tentatively put its makeshift mouth to the rim of the cup. The liquid threatened to spill over, but the creature controlled the movement. I felt their surprise as they tasted the drink.

They passed the cup back to me and paused as the drops filtered down their translucent body. Its mouth smiled as their head nodded. Apparently, they'd learned a lot about the human body from our three-day fuck-fest.

I took another drink, already feeling strength coming back into my limbs.

"That is so fucking cool." One of our observers in the control room exclaimed.

Another piped up from the background. "Oh, and we were able to reroute Edward and Stacey back to their outpost. You won't have to hear them lecture you about your unorthodox ways and the needless risks you take."

"Thank you." Damian and I said in unison.

"Or their lack of proper clothing." One of the people off screen said. "Personally, I like watching their naked bits. Makes it interesting."

Before either Damian or I could respond, tension swept through the mass. I switched one of the screens displaying our health data to our station surveillance system to view the external sensors, just as they sounded a warning about an approaching object. It seemed to be that same multi-craft mass that we'd been watching before the space bugs arrived.

This time, it wasn't just passing by. It was heading straight for us.

"Can you feel their fear?" I asked Damian. "Whatever is coming must be some sort of predator to them."

Damian nodded. He finished his drink and stood before the controls. Unlike last time, when he readied our defense, I didn't stop him.

Within minutes, the mass came into view.

They were creatures, not spaceships, as we'd assumed. Each one was about the same size as a horse, only much more agile. Like the bugs, they didn't have discernible limbs, but they did have eyes and mouths. In the glow from the station's lights, they looked like demons, hovering outside our outpost. They seemed to converse with each other about how best to get to the bugs, which clearly seemed to be their target. A quick glance at the outside cameras showed there were only a few bugs left out there as lookouts. Most had found their way into our outpost.

I did my best to soothe their fear and hoped they'd find a way to tell me what these things were and how to get rid of them.

Before I could get any answers, the creatures outside began to batter our station. Each one accelerating toward our hull even though I couldn't detect any form of propulsion.

The alarms sounded more urgently, letting us know that whatever they were, they were damaging the outer hull of our outpost.

I instructed the computer to record the attack and search for similar occurrences. We had to stop these creatures before they killed us.

There was a surge of determination from the tiny creatures as their fear turned to anger. Then a physical exodus as the space bugs seeped out through our station's hull toward their foe.

We watched in horror as the larger creatures began hunting our tiny friends. It was chaotic.

I felt their pain as each creature succumbed to injuries sustained from the demon-like horde. Yet, they surrounded their predators and closed in. We watched as they changed to wisps, and the herd of attackers began to writhe in obvious pain before turning into space dust.

The battle took only seconds.

We ignored our system's screeched warnings of outer hull breaches, as we watched the surviving space bugs reform into a much smaller mass.

I felt their relief and then another surge of intent.

Once they regrouped, they spread themselves out over the damaged parts of our hull. It took only minutes before, one at a time, the warning lights began going out as the bugs repaired the breaches.

When they finished, they poured back inside and surrounded us. I could feel an ephemeral tugging at the edge of my consciousness. A slight drain on my newly replenished energy.

"Damian, we need more of these nutrition-blasts. They're injured."

Damian and I ran to the food unit and began guzzling the smoothies as fast as we could.

It didn't take long for us to sense their increased energy reserves as they replenished through us. Our new friends felt as good as new. Except there were far fewer of them after their battle with their predators.

It didn't take long for their feelings of well-being to turn to arousal again.

Damian looked over at me with a smirk. "What do you think, Elin? One more for the road?"

The sneaky little creatures were already stroking my body, making it hard for me to refuse. I widened my stance, giving them access to my cunt as they massaged every inch of my skin. I looked over to where our crew on earth were still monitoring us and smiled. "See you in a few days."

MAELSTROM

DAMIAN

Elin and I were standing just inside the entryway, waiting for the Ambassador to arrive.

We had trouble keeping the smiles off our faces because we knew we were in for a treat. The Hooya were the ones to arrange this visit, and we all knew what that meant.

We assured them we would welcome the Ambassador with open... everything.

I have to admit, our reaction wasn't particularly mature when we first saw a picture of the Ambassador's species.

It resembled something my niece would proudly display on the refrigerator at her grandmother's house. Spindly arms and legs with gigantic hands and feet. It had a single round ball for a body that also was its head, with its mouth sliced through the middle. It had googly eyes that protruded upwards from its head slash body like flowers suspended on long stems. Its nose perched precariously on top. The bridge of the nose was long and narrow and stuck up like a blunt horn that had been slicked back with styling gel. It had just one nostril.

Elin stood beside me. I could feel her eagerness. Her movements were subtle enough that the station's scanners didn't pick up how she shifted her hips to rub her legs together.

It didn't matter that we'd had sex less than an hour ago to calm our excitement. It had been a while since we had a scheduled alien rendezvous.

47

Sure, we had some adventures, but the gnome and the space bugs hadn't been scheduled. They appeared out of nowhere and caught us by surprise. As fun as those encounters were, they didn't have the same build-up of anticipation.

Our incoming guest, or should I say in-cumming guest, had been told everything about our physiology.

But to increase the air of mystery, the Hooya refused to tell us anything about the Ambassador's sexual preferences. Our friend, Ina, just smiled, winked and told us to enjoy ourselves.

Finally, the door slid open, and our guest arrived.

Even though we knew his statistics from our database, he was shorter than I was expecting. The top of his body came barely up to my waist. It was the size of a basketball. His arms extended from each side and his legs from below. His body was both torso and head just like in the picture, just below where his arms attached, his mouth sliced across his chest area. It extended from one side to the other and was surrounded by big, puffy lips that looked like a Botox injection gone wild.

His eyes suspended above his head on flexible stalks that moved around constantly, giving him a 360-degree view. They retracted and extended almost half a meter above the rest of him, giving him the ability to see over my shoulder despite his short stature.

I couldn't help but wonder what his mouth and those lips would feel like wrapped around my cock.

My niece would have been disappointed that he wasn't green or purple.

He was a boring brownish-black, like a tabby cat or raccoon. He wore no clothing. The fur around his mouth and over the top of his head/body was short and very soft looking. The hair on his underside was longer and hung like a skirt covering where his legs protruded.

I barely could keep myself from laughing as I took in the size of his hands and feet as I remembered Elin's joking comment earlier.

"We all know what big hands and feet mean, don't we?"

He was accompanied by a tall, graceful figure. It was hard to see what they looked like because they were draped in heavy fabric from head to toe and towered over the Ambassador. Their presence was unexpected and a little odd, considering the carnal intent of the meeting.

The Ambassador spoke in rumbling gurgle sounds that made the station's translator pause.

It made a few clicks that sounded like index cards in an old-fashioned library catalogue, which I had programmed in one day when I was bored, so we'd know the computer was still processing. Then the station said, "We're sorry. We cannot decipher the words from our sound archives. We cannot translate."

Crap, now what do we do? I thought to myself. Charades can only go so far.

"Allow me to interpret. Ours is a tonally nuanced language, which is difficult for most artificial translating systems."

"Of course, thank you for your help." Elin said. "May I ask who you are? We were only expecting the Ambassador."

"I am a facilitator. In our culture, my species is a background entity devoted to ensuring the Ambassador's visit goes smoothly. I am honoured to be here." The draped figure paused. "In your tongue, call me Faci."

"Faci the facilitator?" I couldn't help smiling. It reminded me of the alliteration in the names of many children's characters, like Bob the Builder, and Tony the Tetratonic.

"The Ambassador says he is pleased to be here. The Hooya have spoken highly of you."

"We hold them in high regard as well." Elin said. "We have been told very little about the Ambassador. We will leave the procedure for this encounter in your hands."

Faci bowed slightly. "He appreciates the trust you have bestowed upon him. I will not participate, as it's forbidden in our culture. I will serve merely to aid with translation and positioning, if necessary."

Elin and I looked at each other. I'm sure hers wasn't the only raised eyebrow.

"Do not fear, the Hooya have trained us well in your physical preferences and limitations. It will be enjoyable." There was humour in their voice. "Shall we begin?"

"Yes, please." Damian and I said like chorusing five-year-olds.

"The Hooya suggested to us that Damian should sit on the chair at the main computer station, and Elin should lean back against the keyboards in front of him." They paused. "After you reroute the controls from that area to prevent any mishaps, of course."

The Ambassador followed behind us, rubbing his hands together. No words were necessary. He was eager to get started.

I sat on the wide chair and started to lower the armrests as Elin and I often did before having sex. It gave her room to be on top without bashing her knees.

Faci stopped me. "You'll need those."

Intrigued, I refastened the safety latch, put my arms on the rests. I let my legs fall open as Faci flipped the control on my chair to slide it back along the floor as far as it could from the computer. I was already hard. My cock throbbed and seemed to grow even more rigid as Faci motioned Elin into position.

She was standing in front of me but leaning away. Her ass rested against the ledge of built in keyboards. This put over half a meter between the front edge of my seat and her legs.

Before I could wonder about the distance, the Ambassador stood between us. To my surprise, he faced me instead of Elin.

His large hands grasped the underside of my thighs and pulled me toward him until my ass teetered on the edge of the cushion.

I felt the back of the chair suddenly release behind me as Faci moved me to a reclining position. I had to wrap my arms around the armrests to keep from sliding to the floor.

The Ambassador wrapped his arms around my legs and lifted my butt from the chair. The soft hair on his body tickled the inside of my thighs. He used his oversized hands to massage my ass as he pulled me closer.

A twinge of fear ran through me. I'd never been in such a vulnerable position before. I was powerless in this pose, with my feet dangling down the Ambassador's back, thighs caught under his arms, and the bulk of my weight resting on my shoulders. I was immobile.

He said something to Faci, in his gurgle-y language.

"The Ambassador will start now. Please let him know if anything displeases you or causes you discomfort."

"Discomfort?" My voice went up an octave. What the fuck was this guy going to do to me?

"Relax," Faci soothed. "He is being overcautious. He understands that pain and pleasure thresholds are different for each human. He wishes only pleasure for you both."

I nodded my agreement to the Ambassador.

His smile was wide. He let out a gurgle that sounded satisfied and then stuck out his tongue toward me. It extended past his lips by a full hand's length and was nearly the width of my palm. It stroked from my anus, over my balls and curled itself lengthwise around my shaft and gave my dick a gentle squeeze as it went from root to tip.

"Fuck, that feels good."

The Ambassador made another satisfied gurgle and did it again before leaning down and wrapping his lips around my cock.

The suction was exquisite as his tongue continued to jerk me off within the hot confines of his mouth.

I moaned and began to thrust.

He backed off slightly.

Was it to tease me? Each time I moved forward; he released his tongue's grip on my rock-hard cock.

I forced myself to stop moving, waiting to see what he'd do next.

Once I stilled, he started again. He did this over and over to me. Sucking my cock and then holding back. It was the best kind of torture. His tongue extended past his lips and engulfed my balls in its wet heat. It was broad and flexible enough that it kept hold of my cock while massaging my balls and pressing delightfully against the tender flesh behind them.

If my eyes had been open, he'd be able to see them rolling back in my head.

My glutes tensed with the urge to thrust forward. I stuck my ass out to keep myself immobile. He started circling my opening with one of his balloonish fingers. As soon as I relaxed my ass, his somehow already lubed finger popped in past my sphincter and filled me with one quick thrust, followed by the most amazing feeling.

His digit was long and thick. The bump of his knuckles sent shivers up my spine as it moved in rhythm with his mouth on my cock.

He was holding me up with his hands, which meant he could twist and turn me however he wanted, to aid him in accessing every nook, cranny and nerve ending.

From the waist down, I was one huge, erogenous zone. Even my toes pulsed in time with each stroke of his tongue as he sucked me off.

Elin gasped.

I'd almost forgotten about her. I turned my head to look past the Ambassador to see his eyeballs flexing behind him on their stalks, rubbing their backs against her breasts or fluttering their eyelashes over her nipples. To my surprise, his nose was no longer perched on the top of his body. Instead, it stretched out on a thick trunk, and its horn-like bridge was fucking her with the same rhythm he was sucking me. The nostril flared every time it slapped against her pussy lips.

"Do not worry, he is eager to satisfy you in this manner as well." Faci said as they held up one of Elin's legs to give the Ambassador more room to play.

Fuck, the way he was pounding Elin made my ass clench and bear down on his finger as it worked inside me, bringing me to the point of cumming.

He sensed my approaching climax and eased his ministrations just enough to make the urge to orgasm pass, and then started his combination of suction and jerking me off with his tongue all over again, expertly making me teeter on the edge of ecstasy.

Elin let out another gasp as she fell back onto the computer displays.

Faci helped to hold her steady, so she didn't fall to the ground as her knees gave out. Faci may not have been allowed to participate sexually, but they seemed to be enjoying themself as they assisted the Ambassador by acting as a prop for Elin.

Elin's orgasm set off my own as the grip of the Ambassador's tongue around my cock circled swiftly like a maelstrom of suction and pleasure.

I only hoped the Hooya had warned him about human ejaculation. I swear I couldn't stop cumming as wave after wave shot down his throat.

Finally, the Ambassador raised his head.

His eyeballs rose from where they rested on Elin's chest, blinked rapidly and moved around our bodies, exploring our satisfaction from every angle.

His nose shrank back to perch at the top of his body again, still wet from Elin's arousal.

He said something in their language to Faci, who translated for us.

"When you have recovered sufficiently, the Ambassador would like you to switch positions. He is curious to experience all the differences between the male and female of your species."

"A moment please, before we continue." Elin walked over to the small area off to the side. "Would you or the Ambassador like food or beverage?"

It seemed the Ambassador understood our language but couldn't speak it. He responded to Faci. They replied. "No, neither of us require sustenance in the same way as humans. We are fine."

After a couple of clicks at the machine, Elin picked up two small smoothies. She handed one to me.

As soon as Elin and I finished our drinks, we decided we were rested enough to forge ahead. Eager to see what else the Ambassador had up his sleeve. Well, his imaginary sleeve, since he was as naked as we were.

Elin sat on the chair I'd just vacated to watch as Faci followed the Ambassador's instructions on how to position me.

When they finished, I was bent over, facing the same computer bank Elin had been leaning against. My back was arched to make my ass stick up in the air, as if eagerly waiting to be penetrated by the Ambassador's thick nasal appendage.

Oh wait, it was.

Elin giggled. "Damian, wait until you feel the way his nose moves. Oh my God, it is divine."

Once we were in position, Faci asked, "Are you ready for round two?"

Amelia Dax

We both nodded. "Yes, please." Apparently, we were getting very good at speaking in unison. I'm sure it helped that we were of like mind and couldn't wait to get started.

I looked over my shoulder and watched Elin's expression as she got the first feel of the Ambassador's tongue against her cunt.

He did the same to her as he'd done to me. He began with one long lick from her ass to her clit. His hands were already under her, holding her up, and his thumbs gently parted her vagina's outer lips to get to the heart of her arousal.

She sighed as his tongue rolled lengthwise to enter her like a cock. Her eyes rolled back in her head as I imagined the tip of his tongue wiggled back and forth on the inside of her channel, teasing her in a way no human penis could never imitate. "Oh, my God. So good." she exclaimed.

I was so enraptured by watching her I barely noticed the nudge of the Ambassador's eyeballs as they spread apart my butt cheeks. I twisted as far as I could to watch. It was a bit unnerving to see the Ambassador's eyes act like an extra set of hands. My already hard dick grew even harder as its nose rose up on its thick stem and came toward me.

The bridge lengthened and thick knuckle-like ridges appeared. It gave a couple of quick sneeze-like gestures, which added to Elin's barely dry juices and made it glisten.

My cheeks clenched in anticipation before I forced them to relax to make entry easier.

As it penetrated me, I realized it wasn't as rigid as it looked. Like his fingers, it seemed to be jointed in several places, allowing it to flex inside me.

As I got used to how it felt, it seemed to move purposefully, as if testing my limits.

56

I stopped looking over my shoulder at Elin. My head dropped down and rested on the top one of the computer displays. I closed my eyes to focus on the way it felt to get fucked by the Ambassador's nose at the same time he was tonguing Elin into oblivion.

It moved more forcibly, in and out of my asshole, until he was pounding me just as hard as he'd done Elin.

It felt like someone had connected an electric current to every part of my body and turned it on to maximum strength.

His eyes, having completed their task of holding my butt cheeks out of the way, moved around my body and began stroking my shaft in tandem. They rubbed up and down my cock and then teased my balls, with almost feather like kisses from their eyelashes as they blinked rapidly against my sac.

When we were kids, we used to joke around about getting fucked in the eyeball, but never about being fucked by an eyeball. It was the strangest concept, but the best sensation. I knew I wouldn't last long, even though I'd come hard less than ten minutes ago.

Elin's gasps echoed what I was feeling.

It seemed all the Ambassador's appendages were in sync to fuck and suck us like a well-orchestrated masterpiece. Matching rhythms pulled us towards orgasm and then they'd back off and then they'd bring us close to the brink again.

My balls drew up tight against me and I was going to explode if I didn't cum soon.

This was some serious tantric shit, and the Ambassador showed no sign of stopping and I didn't want him to. I could ride this wave forever, or at least until my body gave out.

Like last time, Elin was the first to let go. She screamed long and loud as I heard the Ambassador still slurping at her soaked pussy.

Suddenly the Ambassador's nose withdrew from my ass despite me clenching my butt to hold him in. A split second later, I felt a firm grip on my cock just as I started to ejaculate.

I opened my eyes to see the Ambassador's nose had come in front of me and was now snorting my dick as cum jettisoned out of my balls, making my knees weak.

Absently, I realized Faci was beside me, straddling the Ambassador's extended appendages and holding my hips steady so I didn't collapse and crush his nasal stalk against the computer station.

Her touch was gentle, but strangely neutral. She didn't enhance the experience, and she didn't take away from it either. I watched my cock soften and slide out of the lone nostril that now had a dribble of my cum hanging from the end.

It gave one sharp sniff, and the cum disappeared up into its nose.

Faci deftly stepped aside, her legs obviously longer than I thought, allowing the Ambassador's nose to settle again on his head. They translated his happy gurgling noise, "He said you are both delicious. Good to the last drop."

I looked over at Elin. She was still on the chair, her limbs hanging limply. "I can't move, but I want to do it again."

Faci said, "He doesn't have time, this trip. But the Ambassador would like to visit you both again if you are amenable." She held out her hand to aid Elin up to a sitting position.

This time it was me who prepared the nutritional booster drink for us and handed one to Elin.

She was still holding Faci's arm, but no longer for support. It seemed as if the two were deep in conversation, though neither spoke a word.

Rather than call them out, I re-evaluated the Ambassador's appearance. He was no longer comical or cartoonish. Knowing what each of his appendages was capable of had me observing him with new respect.

He must have sensed my curiosity. He stepped forward and lowered his body as if bowing. His eyeballs extended toward me and nudged my hands.

I couldn't understand what he said, but his gurgle-y voice sounded encouraging.

Without breaking their connection with Elin, Faci said, "Please go ahead. The Ambassador knows you must be curious."

With that, I cradled his eyes in my hand as I would the back of an infant's head.

Its lashes fluttered in contentment.

I stroked my fingers across the ridged skin down to where the stalk holding the eyeball began.

The Ambassador's entire body shook with pleasure. Even I recognized the guttural sound that came from his lips. His nose began ascending on its thick trunk. The bridge lengthened as if it were getting an erection. So, I jerked it off gently and felt it grow thicker under my touch.

No wonder I'd felt so full. It was fucking huge.

I reached with my other hand to the trunk below and moved my hands in unison.

On my third stroke, his nose splattered all over me.

It was enough to break Faci from their silent conversation with Elin. "Apologies." They pulled out a large cloth from somewhere within their head-to-toe draping and handed it to the Ambassador.

As he patted me dry, Faci explained. "He was not prepared for the feel of your hands on his…" She paused as if searching for a word and then just pointed. "That." Their hand dropped. "It is the most sensitive and vulnerable part of his body, usually only touched during the mating process."

"So, Damian is pregnant?" Elin's joke broke the embarrassed tension coming from the Ambassador.

"No." Humour was also evident in Faci's voice. "But it's usually difficult for a male of the species to ejaculate and Damian made it happen with only a few touches."

"We seem to have that effect on some species." I chuckled. "The Hooya are pro-creating like rabbits, thanks to a little human participation."

Faci and the Ambassador nodded to acknowledge my statement. Faci said. "This we know. The Hooya have made it known that you are integral to their species and therefore under their protection. The Ambassador was honoured to have been chosen to meet you."

"You mean there is a waiting list?" Elin was as shocked as I was. Then her expression changed to one of anger. "Are the Hooya profiting from our…" she struggled for a word. "services?"

"Not as you are assuming." Faci raised their hand as if to halt our wrong impression. "The Hooya are creating a network of those willing to keep humans safe from species who are not interested in peace. The Ambassador is powerful among several allied worlds."

"So, they're making sure each of them has a personal reason to keep us safe."

"Yes." Faci bowed low. "Damian and Elin, you are more important that you understand to the survival of your planet."

With that, they turned toward the exit portal. Just as they were about to go through, the Ambassador bowed low and said something in his language. Awe still tinged his tone.

Faci did one final translation. "He is deeply grateful for having spent this time with you. He pledges to do everything in the power of his people, and those in his care, like my species, to ensure your health and prosperity."

They stepped back, and the doors closed, blocking them from our view.

"Hey guys," Elin got the attention of our monitoring crew on Earth.

"That was beyond words." One of the guys back on our home planet said. "I came three times just watching."

"Yeah, yeah. I'm glad you enjoyed the show." I interrupted. I could tell something was troubling Elin. We could rehash the particulars of our experience later.

"Is what he said true? Are humans in danger?" she asked.

The two people in the room shared a look. "Technically yes. You knew that when you agreed to be part of the Outpost Program."

"Danger was presented as an abstract idea, and you know it." She scolded. "Is there a real threat?"

Back on Earth, they shared another look. "There is chatter, but nothing definite yet."

"Thanks." she said before breaking the video connection.

"So, we're fucking aliens to save the planet now." I asked to confirm what we'd just learned.

"I guess so." Her expression was sober and then it lightened up. "Good thing we're good at it."

I laughed with her, relieved the somber moment had passed. "We should probably get cleaned up. You go first. I'll re-engage the computer station we used."

"You're the best, Damian." She said as she walked down the hall to her quarters.

Later, as we were eating, Elin said with a smile, "Faci lied." Her grin grew bigger at the juicy secret she was about to impart. "They said their species were forbidden to participate. The Ambassador doesn't know they're an Empathic species. They felt every thrust, every lick and every orgasm."

"Is that why they were draped?"

"Possibly." She shrugged. "Empathetic communication is mostly emotional with flashes of images. It can't really discuss details."

We sat in silence and finished our meal.

As I stood to clear our dishes, I said. "I wonder who our next benefactor will be?"

Elin returned my grin. "I can't wait to find out."

ROTHRENGAL

ELIN

Elin and I have been fucking around all morning to quell some of the sexual excitement as we watched the Rothrengal ship come closer. The last thing I wanted to do was blow my load as soon as the alien walked into our outpost.

Even though I just jerked off a few minutes ago, I'm sporting a full mast once again. If the shuttle from the Rothrengal emissary ship wasn't about to land, I'd give in to the urge to plow into Elin's tight pussy. Hell, I was so excited the breeze from the doors sliding open could probably set me off.

The Rothrengal had been Earth's first contact with aliens from another planet. According to their logged history, they came to Earth around what we now call 250AD.

It was a coordinated effort among their allied planets to explore the newest branches of the universe after it had cooled sufficiently for them to deem it habitable. They were looking for new life forms in the developing galaxy we call home.

Earth was in the section the Rothrengal had been assigned. They observed our planet for a while and decided it was best to approach two emerging civilizations: The Mayans and the Romans. From what they had seen, theirs were the largest and most advanced cultures at the time.

The Mayans weren't very receptive.

They thought the Rothrengal, with their penis shaped bodies, were monsters. Demons from the Xilbalba. The Mayans greeted them with warriors.

The Rothrengal's emissaries were not equipped to fight, so they were slaughtered.

As a warning to others and a display of pride at successfully thwarting what the Mayans considered an invasion, they immortalized the alien's defeat by burying their bodies. Leaving only their phallic shaped head above ground encased in stone. Then they built a temple over the graveyard to glorify the event.

The Romans were much more receptive. They were already a horny bunch, eager to find pleasure wherever they could.

One glance at the Rothrengal's phallic shaped bodies had them welcoming the alien emissaries with open arms and legs. They immortalized the visit by creating statues to honour them and wore talismans bearing images of the Rothrengal around their necks.

The Rothrengal became stuff of legends and the basis for several porn empires through the centuries that followed.

Elin had been studying their ancient texts as part of her training.

The Rothrengal were a species devoted to sex in all its forms. They had short sturdy legs with long thick penis shaped bodies that balanced on their legs at a forty-five-degree angle, like a lopsided teeter-totter. The top of their bodies curved up slightly toward the head. Instead of arms, they had small wings on either side which fluttered to help them balance. Necessary because the mushroom shape of their head made them top heavy.

They had no face, which was probably what freaked out the Mayans. Like a penis, they had just a slit, vertically across the top, which seemed to act as a blowhole for breathing, a mouth for speaking and, from the texts Elin had studied, where they blew their load when they were super-stimulated.

To further help their balance, they had a tail that was also a long penile shape with a bulbous head, which could extend in any direction but normally lay curved over their back. Their last appendage hung between their legs and yes, you guessed it; it was another giant penis. This one, like the tail, was a more human-friendly size.

Not wanting to affect how our civilization progressed, they mostly stayed away except for contact with a small group of people. To the public, they became mythical creatures, while, in the background, they helped prepare us to meet other alien cultures, who now regularly passed through our little slice of the heavens.

Even though the Rothrengal were the instigators for us to meet The Hooya and most other species we've encountered, neither Elin or I had ever met a Rothrengal in person.

That was about to change though, because their key emissary to Earth was making a special trip to our outpost. He felt it was time to meet the wonder-kids of interstellar Earth relations.

In other words, the insatiable Damian and Elin.

Us, he was here to meet us.

It was kind of weird to realize that we were interstellarly semi-famous. I mean, we knew we had a cult following on Earth. There was footage from our encounters unofficially leaked by official channels. Their goal was to help lessen the fear most Earth people still held about alien encounters.

A little wariness was a good thing, but total and unnecessary fear of encountering other forms of life was counterproductive to everything the Rothrengal and Hooya were trying to accomplish.

They sought to protect us. They wanted human beings to thrive as a species in interstellar space. For all intents and purposes, humans were their pet project.

So, if leaking video of Elin and I having sex with different alien species helped to make the idea of aliens more palatable to the public, of course, we'd willingly make the sacrifice.

His shuttle had just completed the docking process and our first up close and personal contact with the famed Rothrengal was about to happen.

The station kept us informed of his progress along the pressurized corridor to our door. My attention was torn between watching for the doors to slide open and the feeling of my pre-cum sliding along the underside of my cock and onto my balls.

I knew the Rothrengal would view my excitement as a compliment.

Endless minutes later, he walked through our door.

Even though he technically had no face to smile, I didn't need to be an empath like Elin to feel his elation at being with us.

As was their custom, he bowed low, the mushroom top of his head nearly touching the floor in front of him.

Elin and I bowed as well.

The sticky spot of pre-cum from the tip of my cock spread to my abs. As I straightened, it formed a long line of viscous cream until it snapped when I stood up. Leaving the long strand swinging in the gentle breeze as the doors swished shut behind our guest.

The slit at the top of the Rothrengal's head vibrated as he spoke. His words were unintelligible to the human ear, but our station found it easy to translate. After all, they were the first alien language programmed into the system.

"I have been looking forward to meeting the two of you for a very long time."

"It's lovely to finally meet you too," Elin said with an enormous smile on her pretty face that lit up her eyes, which were mischievously gleaming as I'm sure she thought about the plan we'd come up with, to rock the Rothrengal's world.

He spoke again, and the station translated. "I regret my time here is so short and we must forgo the normal pleasantries expected in polite human society."

Elin and I looked at each other and grinned. "As you may have heard, we're not so traditionally polite."

The satisfied grunt that came through his blowhole needed no translation.

Elin guided him down the hallway toward one of the guest chambers. The position she wanted to try required a soft, flat surface. She led us into the room with a large bed in the center and large mirrors attached to the walls at the head of the bed and on either side.

Hmm, those were new. She'd been busy redecorating during my last sleep cycle.

"I've studied your texts and thought about a position that will satisfy all three of us." She told our guest. "Damian will be under you so you can ride him doggy style. I'd straddle your back and you can fuck me with your tail. She paused. "If that is acceptable to you?"

67

The Rothrengal nodded quickly in agreement.

Elin and I had already discussed our strategy earlier, so I immediately got on the bed and positioned myself on all fours, and then stuck my ass in the air.

With Elin's hand steadying him as he climbed on top of the mattress, she steered him to stand behind me, lowering himself slightly until the underside of his cock shaped body rested over my back and his erect cock wedged lightly in my crack.

He seemed to like it so far because he immediately lubricated my buttocks with a dollop of pre-cum.

Once she was certain the Rothrengal was stable, she helped our guest run his penis up and down between my ass cheeks. She eased him back to let the tip of his penis drop below my body and massage my balls as his cock poked between my legs and rubbed lengthwise against mine. It was a glorious sensation. His skin was soft as he cradled my balls in the apex between his shaft and body. We started moving together.

"Let me know when you're ready for me." Elin said as she stroked both of our cocks.

I could feel the breeze from his wings fluttering as he backed up to have room for the tip of his penis to poke my puckered asshole. I could feel the cool wet pre-cum as he smeared it back and forth, then gently pushed forward, past my sphincter, and up into my channel.

"Fuck." I let out my breath as I tried to relax around him. "You feel fantastic." It was true, I'd never felt so full.

He was longer and wider than a human. He went slowly, allowing my body to adjust as I moved back and forth and side to side. Arching and bowing my back to better accommodate him.

He pulled out and then pushed in a little further. Oozing more pre-cum into my channel, until eventually he was in as far as he could go. I could feel our balls knocking together between my legs.

Selfishly, I wanted to forget about Elin, but I know she had a vital role to play in the Rothrengal's pleasure.

For them to truly be satisfied, all three of their penis appendages needed to be stimulated in order to have a Climax-Divinus, a simultaneous orgasm. It was the only way for their large body-cock to ejaculate. It was the pinnacle of ecstasy for the Rothrengal.

A single human couldn't do it. Truthfully, it may not be possible with just the two of us, but we were going to give it our best effort.

I pressed my shoulder blades together to help hold him steady and nodded to Elin. "Okay, we're ready." I turned my head to look over my shoulder to watch her swing her leg over his back. Her legs were barely long enough to touch her toes on the mattress on either side of his girth.

She stretched her body up along the top of his, then reached around to the underside of his mushroom head. She leaned forward and tilted her hips so his tail could moisten itself with her pussy juices before easing into her entrance.

Her gasp made my balls tighten.

In the mirror, I could see her eyes roll back in her head as his cock tail moved like a snake, easing in and out, testing the limits of her snatch. Its length was triple that of a normal penis. It pushed its way in until it could go in no further.

"Holy Fuck." Elin put her arms just under his glans, spreading her fingers until she found the spot she was looking for.

The one that made the Rothrengal's entire body shiver. He flapped his wings to help keep him in position.

"Oh, my God." she exclaimed. "His feathers feel awesome against my tits."

With everyone in position, we started to move. Slowly, at first, until we found our rhythm and settled into a synchronized motion.

He plunged into me and, as he backed off, he arched his lower body to plunge his tail into Elin.

With each stroke, her arms tightened around the large mushroom head of his body, massaging the sensitive frenulum just under his glans with her fingers.

I tilted my head back, letting my hair glide against the underside of his huge cock head. Providing another touch point of sensation for our guest.

He murmured an appreciation as we continued to rub up against him, me on his underside and Elin and her breasts on the upper. As we rode his cock and cock-tail, the Rothrengal started to move his body faster until he slid in and out of my asshole like a battering ram.

Fan-fucking-tastic.

Elin hung on for dear life. She dug her heels into my hips, trying to find a purchase to hold on to.

Meanwhile, his wings beat furiously to keep him upright. The exertion made each of us a sweaty mess.

My hair was soaked. I didn't know it was from sweat, or if it was the pre-cum dribbling from the slit at the top of his head.

I could feel Elin sliding to one side and then the other as she tried to balance on top of the giant cock jacking itself off between our bodies.

He said something, but his words were gurgled. They became bubbles blown in the lubricant, pooling in his blowhole. It was a wonder he didn't choke on his own sperm.

The pleasure was intense. My ass was on fire in the best way. He was so large. He stretched me past what I thought I was capable of. I felt every ridge as he plunged into me. The thumping rhythm of his balls was like nothing I'd ever felt before.

Elin screamed above me. "Fuck me." Her heels dug into my calves, bracing herself as her body shook with her first orgasm of the night.

Our bodies were almost too slick to keep our positions, which was something we hadn't thought of when we decided on this stance.

As Elin started coming down from her orgasm, she straightened her legs to the mattress, using her thighs to help the Rothrengal hold steady as he continued to pound into me.

His stamina was unbelievable. Even though Elin had slowed her movements, he still hammered away at both of us. It took only seconds for her to recover and start clenching around him again.

I know because I could feel her hips tighten around his body's torso and thus my hips when she did.

Ready to go again, she got back into sync. We had a plan. Our goal was to make the Rothrengal's gigantic mushroom head cum.

It was one of the reasons we chose to have this escapade away from the main control room. Sure, the guys back on Earth were probably pissed at us for denying them real time viewing pleasure, but we had a mission to personally thank the Rothrengal for all they've done for us.

Not just for Earth as a civilization but for all the encounters they've facilitated for us via the Hooya. We wanted to make his big cock cum and shower us with his spunk, which wasn't advisable in the station's main command center.

The Romans claimed it was good luck to make a Rothrengal achieve Climax-Divinus and if what the Ambassador said a few weeks ago was true about malevolent aliens wanting to do us harm, we'd need all the luck we could get.

Elin worked his giant cock head with her hands while she slid her body up and down the length of his. I heard her gasp every time his wings brushed against her breasts.

The under feathers of his wings stroked along my shoulders, adding an extra layer of sensation as I arched my back against the giant cock's rigid vein that pulsed against my skin. The front of his thighs slapped against my ass every time I plunged down over his cock. Every thrust created sparks of friction, making bolts of coloured light explode behind my eyelids.

He was close. His entire body grew taut at the same time my sac tightened.

Elin screamed as her arms and thighs above me spasmed.

I felt the deep rumble along my back an instant before he released a torrent of cum that plastered the wall at the head of the bed with enough force that it dented the metal mirror. He braced his legs and made one more frantic thrust into both of us, setting off a chain reaction.

My jizz exploded out of me. I would have had a mouthful had I not thrown my head back against the Rothrengal's underside as my orgasm ripped through me.

Elin screamed as she clenched her thighs to stay on the Rothrengal's back. Her pussy was so wet, her juices spilled down past my hips.

The Rothrengal was busy trying not to choke on his ejaculation, as he tried to catch his breath while still sandwiched between us. His poor wings were drenched, and his legs trembled as if they couldn't hold him up for much longer.

Elin moved first and slid to the right side of the mattress. "That was incredible." She said as she reached up to stroke the side of the Rothrengal's body.

"Ready?" I asked him. "I'll move to the left and you fall toward Elin.

He gave a huff, almost like a sneeze that cleared his ejaculate from the slit at the top of his head. This time, the station's translator was able to understand what he was saying. "Yes, must rest."

Elin and I helped guide him onto the bed. His wings fluttered and then stilled while his legs stretched out toward the foot of the bed like an exhausted puppy.

"We did it." Elin sounded so proud as she raised her head over the Rothrengal's exhausted body for a high-five.

"We did." I replied.

Then we both laughed when we realized the Rothrengal had raised its wings to high-five us too.

More sounds emitted from him, and the station interpreted. "I am astounded at your ability to achieve Climax-Divinus. Very few have been able to do this feat with just two humans. The norm has always been three or four people. You are indeed worthy of the legends created about you."

"We have legends about us?" Elin's voice squealed like a little girl.

"Yes. The Hooya have proclaimed you possess what you'd refer to as magical powers. Even the Spatium Cimex have told stories of your wondrous empathic energy and how you supported them against their predators."

"Aww. The space bugs were so cute." Elin said.

"Those you call space bugs are a powerful entity. Gaining their favour was an unexpected boost to our defense plan for Earth."

"The Ambassador had been quite blunt about the danger to Earth from some not-so-friendly species." I recognized this wasn't the usual pillow talk after sex, but things weren't normal, and we weren't the one to bring up the topic. "He made it sound like threats were immediate and not as theoretic as we'd been led to believe when we accepted this post."

"The risk to your planet isn't immediate, yet the threat is very real. Earth is unique in its ability to host diverse life forms." His giant cock head was tense beside me. This time, not in a good way. "We feel responsible because it was us who discovered and drew attention to your existence."

"But, if you hadn't, someone else would have and there is no guarantee they would have had our best interests at heart." Elin, ever the empath, soothed.

I added. "Pimping us out to other species isn't a typical endeavor, but it's been a method for doing business on Earth for centuries. Prostitution is Earth's oldest profession."

"I understand your comparison. Be sure, we are not profiting from arranging encounters with you."

"You aren't, but we are." I said. "We are securing your help to protect our planet with sexual exploits instead of money or property."

"Hey Damian," Elin giggled. "That means your cock is worth its weight in gold."

""Both of you are worth far more than gold. More like the weight of Ancfu in the hands of a Tixlardine." The station translated the Rothrengal's response. The Rothrengal's body shook as a sound that I assumed was laughter came out of his slit.

That gave me an idea. "Can I fuck your slit?"

His entire body stilled.

"I don't mean to offend, but is it possible?"

"It can be done. One has to be careful to pull out and step quickly away. The nerves inside my opening are delicate and I can achieve Climax-Divinus much faster."

"Is there anything I can do to enhance the experience for you?" Elin asked.

"As a female, no. I can only be penetrated during this act."

"Is there another hole?" she asked, which made me smile. Elin didn't like being left out, and I knew where she was going with the question.

"At the base of my cock-tail."

Re-energized, Elin jumped up from the bed and ran to her room. It took her only seconds to return, strapping an enormous dildo around her waist. She'd already inserted the secondary piece into her cunt. "Turn so you're laying across the bed." She ordered.

The Rothrengal's wings flapped, raising his huge cock head toward me as his legs shuffled him around enough to step off the mattress and raise his ass toward Elin.

"Can we hurt you like this?" I asked.

"No." he replied. "Be careful. When I orgasm, the discharge has enough force to injure you."

"Noted." I said as I slid my dick up and down the length of his slit. "Ready?"

"Ready?" Elin and the station's translator said in unison.

Elin used her pussy juices to lubricate the length of her fake dong and together we entered the Rothrengal.

He shuddered and his wings beat against his sides, as if aiding our efforts.

I wasn't sure what to expect. Honestly, I'd asked to fuck him on a whim.

The slit at the end of his cock head intrigued me. It was longer than my hand, yet when I slipped inside, its inner walls hugged my dick as snugly as Elin's pussy did.

It didn't take long for us to see that he liked it better when we both entered him at the same time instead of see-sawing back and forth.

He was so tight and the muscles he used to speak felt like I was getting sucked off as I fucked him. This was a great idea.

Elin and I increased our pace. Her moans echoed my pleasure as we double-teamed our newest friend.

It didn't take long before the muscles inside his slit began to tremble with his approaching orgasm.

Despite my cock plugging his blowhole, he let out a scream of warning just as my balls drew up to let go.

I pulled out and landed on the bed beside him. My cock spurting in the same pulsing rhythm as his cannon which let loose with a force that if I hadn't moved out of the way, it would have broken my back as it hurled me against the wall.

Elin collapsed on the Rothrengal's back, content to let him wipe the matted hair from her forehead with his cock-tail.

I'm sure my mouth hung open as it registered how much cum had actually come from his cock head. It was going to take us hours to mop it all up and clean it from where it dripped from the ceiling.

"If you treat everyone we send to you like this, I fear we'll have wars among those vying to be chosen next to enjoy your attentions." The Rothrengal shook with laughter as the station relayed his words.

"Maybe we should start training others to keep up with the demand." Elin said. From the look on her face, I didn't think she was joking.

"This is an excellent suggestion." He said as his wings flapped again, helping him rise to a standing position. "Your commanders were against this method at first. I believe we are changing their minds. Some Earth dwellers have odd notions about purity being desirable. In most other planets, it's merely a stage to leave behind as you reach maturity. It's not meant to be a way to subvert others for control, as often happens on Earth." His wings flapped again, sending a spray of droplets over the bed. "We will be in touch with your Earth's council to create a plan to implement your suggestion."

"Wow." Elin said as the Rothrengal boarded his shuttle to take him back to his ship. "Can you imagine the uproar those recruiting posters will cause?"

"Have Sex, Save the Earth." I suggested.

"Happy Endings For Aliens Prevents Unhappy Endings For Earth," she tossed out.

"Best Job You'll Ever Have." I said. "Because really, what could be better than this?"

"You've got that right." She agreed. "Hmm. I wonder who they're sending to us next?"

NEVDU

ELIN

Damian and I have become sexual adrenaline junkies. While we still enjoyed fucking each other, our alien exploits have become front and center in our minds. We could barely get through our regular tasks without diverting conversations to the Ghost Gnome's chin or how amazing it felt to get fucked by the Rothrengal and then get him off... twice.

Our counterparts back on Earth weren't helping. If we didn't bring up our escapades, they did. Everyone had a favourite incident and our routine maintenance conversations ended up with Damian and I fucking, while the others looked on, called out requests, jerked off, or joined us on their side of the monitors by fucking each other.

There was a waiting list to be on our team. Which was starting to cause friction between the monitoring stations on Earth and amongst the staff at the other Outposts. Some were horrified at what we were doing, while others wanted in on the action.

After the Rothrengal's visit, there had been an unofficial poll sent to the other teams to see if they'd be interested in helping to clear the backlog of aliens who wanted some human-lovin'. The results showed far more were eager to join in than expected.

To be included in the new 'Sex with Aliens 'program, everyone on an Outpost Team had to agree. Both members had to freely want to transition to the extra-friendly welcoming program. This led to a sudden influx of transfer request notices to shuffle staff to accommodate everyone's desires, or lack thereof.

Damian and I were asked to develop a training course to help others create a welcoming atmosphere for their guests. It was a larger undertaking than we first thought. Creating guidelines and safety parameters for sex was duller that you'd think. Except, for the aforementioned breaks where we all got so horny from talking about sex with various aliens, we all just started fucking... meeting adjourned.

It was two weeks, in Earth time, after the Rothrengal's visit before we received notice of a new arrival scheduled for the following day. Damian and I tried to hide our disappointment when we looked up the species in our database. The Nevdu appeared human.

One head, appropriately placed on their shoulders. Two arms and two legs, they were indistinguishable from us. There were no extra-large appendages. The male's cock looked like it was barely two hand widths in length.

Our next visitors seemed so boring after meeting the Rothrengal. Then again, I suppose he was a tough act to follow.

"Geez, they aren't even a pretty colour." I pointed out their greyish skin tone. "How can they be able to protect humans when they're just like us?" I knew I was whining. It just felt that after all the hype about us having sex with aliens, we were being demoted back to humanoids.

"Looks can be deceiving." Damian said as he read through what we playfully call the sex instruction manual about our next encounter. He smiled. "I think you'll enjoy yourself." He said as he shut down the database.

"Why? What did you find?"

"Let it be a surprise." He said, standing with his arms crossed as if blocking access to the system.

"Seriously, I can look it up on my terminal." I pouted.

"But you won't because you like the mystery."

"Some days I wish you didn't know me so well." I rolled my eyes at him and then moved on to our next task. We had a lot to do before they arrived.

The next day, Damian and I stood in our usual positions. We'd long ago abandoned dressing in our uniforms to greet our guests, but with having humanoid looking aliens about to board, I felt strangely naked. For the first time in ages, I was nervous.

I glanced over at Damian and saw tension in his face. "What's wrong?"

"For the same reason I know you're going to enjoy this encounter, I have doubts I can satisfy the female." For the first time, I noticed his shoulders were slumped. "There is more to them than meets the eye, and I'm not sure my cock will suffice."

Until that moment, I thought he was just exaggerating about the species to help me get over my disappointment. This was the first time I'd ever seen him unsure of his abilities. "I'm sure they've studied us too and will have some suggestions or positions they'd like to experiment with."

"I hope so because honestly, I'm not sure I can bring anything to the table for them."

Just then the doors swooshed open and in walked the Nevdu. As expected, they looked like us except their skin was a bluish grey. They also wore no clothes as they entered our station, which allowed us to see the male's penis inflate to a semi as he perused my body.

Damian's did the same as he watched them approach.

Despite the pallor of her skin, the female was beautiful. If it hadn't been for the male's immediate reaction to me, I would have felt inadequate and self-conscious.

They stopped in front of us, males facing females. "It is our pleasure to meet you." They said together. His voice was deep, hers softer.

"It's lovely to meet you, too." I said.

Damian nodded his agreement beside me.

"Would you like some refreshment?" Because they were human-ish, I felt the need to observe social niceties.

The woman smiled. "Not necessary. We are eager to play." She seemed to mumble. Her diction wasn't very clear. Her lips didn't move as she spoke. It was as if she'd had an over-enthusiastic dose of Botox. Her mouth stayed slightly parted, giving her a look of perpetual surprise.

"We were pleased to be the next in line." The male's deep voice rumbled. His lips didn't move, either. "I am Hwan, this is Etter."

"Your English is very good." Damian said. "I feel negligent in not greeting you in your language."

"Don't be." The woman, Etter, reached out to touch his upper arm and then curled her fingers around his bicep. She lifted her other hand to stroke the skin over his shoulder. "You've encountered many new languages in a short time. We had one, with much incentive to learn it well."

"Incentive?" I asked. Ignoring the shot of jealousy that stabbed my heart as she touched Damian.

"Yes." The male stepped forward until his body was flush against mine. All thoughts of jealousy fled my mind. "They chose the couple who spoke the best English to be on this mission of peace to meet you."

"Thank you for your diligence." I smiled at my suitor. "May I?" I asked as I ran my hand over his chest. Marveling at how hot he was to the touch.

He wrapped his arms around me and pulled me closer. His heat surrounded me.

I expected it to make me sweat and become uncomfortable, but he was the perfect temperature. Like a cup of hot chocolate against cold hands in winter. His warmth made me want to cuddle in closer. I stroked my hands up over his shoulders and enjoyed the feeling as his palms skimmed over my ass.

His touch was firm and gentle as he explored my skin. He bent slightly as he curved his fingers behind my knee and lifted my leg. Only then did he tilt his pelvis forward.

I gasped at the touch of his cock against my legs. It felt twice as huge as it'd been when they walked in. It grazed both of my thighs, even with my legs parted.

"Told you, you'd like him." Damian laughed. To his partner, he asked. "Shall we go someplace more comfortable?"

"We have a room set up for all of us." I explained to Hwan. "We enjoy watching each other. Plus, it helps us learn for next time."

Both of the Nevdu nodded. "We appreciate your openness. We have heard conflicting reports about Earth dwellers. I understand now why you are the chosen ambassadors for your planet."

Damian and I looked at each other and laughed. "We didn't plan it, but it worked out that way."

We led our guests down to the same guest chamber we entertained the Rothrengal. No matter how much we cleaned, we still found bits of his dried semen in the cracks of the walls and floor. Not to worry, the bed was clean, and we could still see our reflections despite the dented mirror at the head of the bed.

Damian took Etter to one side of the soft platform, and Hwan and I took the other. It was equivalent to a king-size bed, which would accommodate all four of us with ease.

"Do you have any preferences?" Damian asked Etter. His hand was already massaging the gap between her legs.

She widened her stance and reached for his other hand. When he placed it in hers, she put it on her breast.

"You are so warm." Damian said.

I turned my attention back to Hwan and gasped. He'd stepped back so I could see his erection jutting out in front of him. Instead of his balls hanging below his cock, they seemed to be encased within the length of his penis. He grew in width as well as length. I reached out with both of my hands to hold him.

He stopped me mid stroke and pulled my hands away from his girth. "If you keep doing that, I will not fit."

I looked down again and his balls had each expanded to the size of a child's fist. "Wow."

He kept hold of my hand as he lay down on the bed. "This way will be easier for your physiology. Just be aware once we start, I cannot stop until I am finished. I could harm you if you try to pull away before my release.

"You will be glad to wait for the end." Etter smiled at me. "It is worth it."

Out of the corner of my eye, I saw Damian's shoulders slump again.

Etter saw it, too. "I understand the differences. You also are unique, and I am looking forward to what you can

84

give me that Hwan cannot. Our physiology doesn't allow what you can do."

Damian looked confused. "Like what?"

"You will see." Hwan said. "It's all she talked about on the way here." Then he turned to me. "Come sit on top of me. I want to be inside you."

I straddled Hwan's hips and ran my pussy up and down over his length. The bloated balls within his cock felt amazing as my clit brushed up against them.

"I can't hold myself in much longer. I must be inside before it's too late."

I rose to my knees and eased myself down over his girth, which seemed to have doubled yet again. He felt so good as I slid down over the solid bumps of his balls. They hit every erogenous point they passed, even ones I didn't know I had, making me ignore the momentary discomfort as my inner walls stretched to accommodate him. Once our bodies were completely joined, I felt him grow even wider inside me. It was as if a switch released his bulk. He felt like a balloon inflating. "Holy shit." I gasped and swiveled my hips to help stretch myself around him. But when I tried to pull off so I could plunge down again, I couldn't. He was too big.

"Relax your inner muscles." Etter said. "We do not move in and out as you do. You can go side to side or in circles, but not up and down."

Taking her advice, I rotated my hips back and forth, which gave my natural lubrication a chance to work and loosen the involuntary grip I had on his cock.

"You are all right?" Hwan asked with a concerned expression.

"Yes, I think so." I was so full it was almost uncomfortable. Wait. What's that?

Hwan's dick started pulsating within my channel. The inflated balls inside his prick seemed to rotate and move up and down within his length. He was fucking me without moving his body at all.

Not that I could stay still. My hips swivelled, adding to the sensation.

His hands came up to cup my breasts. His palms were hot. All the while, his balls never stopped moving inside. They continued to grow and soon I was rotating my hips again, this time in a figure eight motion, which seemed to excite him even more.

Etter threw her head back against the mattress as Damian plowed into her cunt. "Ahh yes." She exclaimed as her hips worked in time with Damian's thrusts, welcoming him into her and grabbing his ass to grind him against her clit, which seemed to grow slightly longer and wider until it was almost the size of my big toe.

Curious, I reached over to wrap my fingers around it to see if she had the same inner movement as Hwan. They both watched as I gripped her nub. It swelled under my touch, becoming bright blue as her breath came faster.

Hwan started panting too as I continued to move over him. I clenched tight and his balls went into a frenzy. Instinctively, I still wanted to move up and down, so I ground my clit against his pubic bone. At least that part of our anatomy was the same.

He cried out. I hoped it was ecstasy. "Again." He panted. "Do that again."

I kept playing with Etter and bore down on Hwan. He grew even bigger inside me, as my cunt worked his balls.

I leaned forward, dangling my breast in front of his mouth. Taking the hint, he latched on. His teeth were slightly sharp, but the pain only increased my arousal, making me tighten around him as he moved within me. I jerked myself back and forth over his root until I shattered again. This time, he followed. The blast coated my cervix. Igniting the nerves trying to have their petit morte as another orgasm crashed over me before the first one was done. As he deflated, his balls continued moving, at a slower place, making me cum yet again. This time it was a softer orgasm, but just as wonderful. My inner muscles held him in place until I was spent.

"Ayahhhh." Etter screamed. Frantically bucking against Damian. I was suddenly glad I stopped touching her when I orgasmed, otherwise they would have mangled my hand the way they pounded together.

Instead of collapsing on Hwan like I wanted to, I braced myself up on my elbow to watch Damian's finale. He plunged into Etter's tight pussy as she bucked up toward him with every thrust. I could tell Damian was close. Sure enough, it took only a few more strokes and his movements grew jerky as he unloaded into her.

Damian fell to his elbows over Etter. His cock was still buried to the hilt.

Hwan said something unintelligible to Etter once any of us could speak again. She nodded vigorously. To me, he said. "You reached over to touch Etter. Would you like more?"

Etter was suddenly shy. "We do not go female to female. It is not forbidden, but there is no purpose."

I cocked my head. "I'm sorry. I reached over without thinking."

87

"No, it wasn't bad." Her grey skin turned the same blue as her clit had. I think she was blushing. "I am now curious. Hwan encouraged me to experiment."

"When we were researching your customs, it shocked us at the amount of oral you use in your encounters. It had never been part of our way."

"Our mouths don't have the same mobility as yours and our tongues do not extend. So, we can't please each other female to female except by hand and that's not enough."

"And our mouths can't do much, let alone fit over our males when we are aroused. We seem to have evolved to where oral is not an option."

"I can play with Etter." I said without hesitation. "What will you do since oral isn't an option?" I asked both men.

Damian said. "We'll just jerk off. I want to see his dick in action. I'm fascinated that his balls are inside his cock."

"Okay, let's do this."

Except for Etter, we stood to rearrange ourselves.

Etter moved up to half sit up against the pillows at the head of the bed so she could watch me eat her out.

Damian kneeled on one side of her and Hwan on the other, their already half inflated dicks in their hands.

"Ready?" I asked Etter. Even though it was her request, I wanted to make sure she was up for this. Creating an intergalactic incident wasn't part of the game plan.

"Please." Her smile was huge. Well, as huge as her mouth would allow.

It had been a long time since I'd gone down on another woman. I trailed my nose up the inside of her thigh, light licks tasting her flavour mingled with Damian's semen, which still dribbled out from her. She smelled different. Her scent wasn't unpleasant, just not human.

Despite my recent orgasms, I was already turned on again. I used my thumbs to open her outer lips, then ran my tongue along either side of her channel.

Her hips jerked in response.

"All right?" I asked, raising my head to make sure she was okay.

"Oh, my." Her eyes glowed and her skin blushed, turning more blue than grey. "That feels wonderful."

The guys were paying rapt attention to how my face moved between Etter's legs.

Satisfied, I lowered my head again, this time exploring her crevice with a firmer tongue, sticking it into her hole where her juices were already overpowering the taste of Damian's spunk. A marked improvement. I smiled to myself, remembering the Ghost Gnome's reaction to the bitterness of his jizz.

I didn't raise my head when she began to move again. It was clear she was enjoying my ministrations, especially when I rose an inch to circle her clit. I huffed air as I laughed at the thought that it was big enough that even the most oblivious Earth male would be able to find it.

With that, I latched on and added suction as I flicked my tongue against her tight bundle of nerves. I barely heard her gasp because her legs had tightened over my ears, blocking out everything but her louder sounds of delight and the grunts of the guys as they jerked themselves off.

It didn't take long for her body to clench and her juices to flood into my mouth. She tasted slightly salty, with a sweet tang that was foreign and familiar. I slowed my lapping, bringing her back down to earth… so to speak, after her orgasm.

When I lifted my head, I saw she'd grabbed Damian's cock and was sucking furiously on the head of it. Its tip slender enough to fit between her stiff lips. Damian braced one hand against the headboard as he leaned against Hwan's shoulder. Together, he and Hwan were holding Hwan's balloon shaped cock, rotating their palms over his balls that were visibly moving under their touch.

I could tell Damian was about to blow, but while Hwan's breathing was laboured, he didn't seem to be as close. Without thinking, I leaned up on my elbow and pressed my lips against the tip of his penis. He was so inflated his slit resembled a belly button. I tickled the indentation with my tongue.

Hwan's reaction was immediate. He threw his head back and let out a scream that echoed in the sparse room. His cock hardened and then spewed thick liquid into my waiting mouth.

I took as much as I could before getting out of the way before I drowned. He had huge balls to empty.

Damian erupted an instant later with Etter valiantly trying to swallow his load.

Tears were streaming down her face by the time he finished, but the look of satisfaction in her eyes made it obvious she enjoyed the experience.

We adjourned to the shower.

Damian and I had made some modifications here as well. Instead of the original multiple stall shower, we'd removed the walls to create a cozy enclosure big enough for four, six if we pressed together. By the time we were done, Etter and I had been fucked again, twice.

Damian and I demonstrated one of our favourite positions with him behind, drilling into me with his balls slapping loudly thanks to the acoustics in the room.

Etter and Hwan did a similar position, but they rotated their hips in opposite directions to each other. They exclaimed their pleasure in their native language, which had Damian and I masturbating while we watched. Then we switched partners and did it again.

I wanted to try one more thing with Hwan before they had to leave. Now that I'd seen his cock in action, I had a better understanding of how to make the experience even more enjoyable for him.

Yeah, I know, they weren't nearly as boring as I feared they'd be. That'll teach me not to jump to conclusions.

This time, I asked Hwan to stand with his back against the wall of the shower. I knelt on one side of him and Damian on the other.

Etter clapped her hands with glee and sat on the bench to watch. "Oh Hwan, you get both tongues."

Hwan's hands flattened against the tile of the shower the instant Damian and I brought our mouths to his length.

We took turns licking and sucking along his cock. With every touch, it seemed to grow in width until it was the size of a child's football.

It boggled my mind that I'd been able to handle such a girth without hurting myself. Fuck, he'd felt good though.

Damian and I lapped at Hwan while massaging him with our palms and fingers where our mouths couldn't reach.

When he was almost ready to burst, I nodded for Damian to do the honours.

Damian wrapped his hands around the end of Hwan's balloon cock and kept up his pace while he began sucking and licking the belly-button-like slit at the end.

Hwan's knees locked, as he gave a roar and exploded into Damian's waiting mouth.

Like me, Damian couldn't take it all. He tilted to the side, which mean Etter got splattered with the rest of his cum.

When he was spent. Hwan slid down the wall. His arms limp by his sides. "That was…"

"Spectacular." I finished his sentence.

Etter, Damian, and I quickly rinsed off and then helped Hwan to his feet. All three of us soaped him up and washed down his exhausted body.

Etter explained as we cleaned up, it was rare for their species to have sex more than once a day. The amount of fluid expelled each time meant the males needed more recovery time. Four times in such a short period would be the stuff of legends.

"Another installment in the Damian and Elin, Earth Ambassador Mythology." Damian joked as we led them back to the greeting area.

"Hey, why do you get to come first?" I complained.

"Because I always make sure you cum first in other ways." He winked at me, and our guests just laughed at our silliness.

"Fair enough." Really, I couldn't argue with his logic. He never finished without me.

When we reached the doors, Damian offered to help Hwan down the hall.

"I've got him." Etter said as she wrapped her arm around her partner. "Thank you, both. This was better than either of us could have hoped for."

"You exceeded all expectations, too." I told them. "I thought you were just going to be boring humans."

"You are human." Hwan said sincerely. "There is nothing boring about you."

With that, he and Etter turned and stepped through the doors.

We watched them leave, noting poor Hwan's legs were still shaky as he leaned heavily against Etter.

"Well?" Damian asked, as they disappeared around the corner.

"You had nothing to worry about after all, eh?" I teased.

"Honestly, after seeing how their males looked during arousal, I figured the female's anatomy would have to be large enough to accommodate. I thought I'd be as arousing as a pebble rolling down a hallway."

"She definitely seemed to enjoy herself." I wrapped my arm around his waist as we walked back into the station's main control area. "We did good."

NYOKA

DAMIAN

Elin and I sat in our chairs while working at the station's controls, vigilant for any anomalies. Ever since the visits from the Ambassador and the Rothrengal, she and I have been on high alert.

Not the station, nor the official threat level, just us.

After all, we were the ones out here in the middle of nowhere. We're the ones who had every alien species' attention and if something went wrong, we were the ones who would have to handle whatever came our way.

Being famous for our sexual escapades was fun for a while, but now there was this underlying edge of worry about everything we did.

Regardless of our wariness, the sex has been fantastic. Nothing like wondering if today is your last to live to make a person feel hyper aware of every kiss, lick and sensation of sliding into her tight cunt or someone sliding into me.

Yeah, the sex was off the charts.

As if my thoughts jinxed the calm, the station's warning system rang out. We had a breach.

Elin frantically searched the monitors to see what the sensors had picked up.

"Warning. Breach of loading dock space side doors." The station's voice boomed.

"There's nothing there." I could hear the panic in her voice. "I can feel something's near, but I can't see anything."

94

"Are you sure?" I asked as I stared at the screens in front of me. "Station, what did you see?"

"All is clear. The breach has resolved itself. No intruder detected."

"Maybe the Ghost Gnome came back to visit." I joked to Elin. Trying to lighten the tense mood in the room.

"He doesn't set off the alarms until he's chin deep in my twat." Her sarcasm had an edge of fear to it. "I know I'm just being paranoid, but I'm not sure I trust the station's effectiveness to monitor for unexpected visitors. It was useless detecting the Space Bugs, too." She paused. "No offence Station."

"None taken, Elin. Indeed, we could not detect the Spatium Cimex." The robotic monotone answered.

"There is nothing there." I pointed to the monitor showing several images of the area where the breach supposedly had occurred. "We have an all clear."

"You folks okay up there?" Faces appeared on the communications portal. "We saw a breach."

"There's nothing here, and I don't see anything on replay."

We watched while our team back on Earth checked their equipment to see if they could find the source of the problem. "There is a slight change in the ratio between inside and outside atmosphere. It seems there was an opening. But for the size of the door, the readings don't match the changes we would have expected unless it opened only a centimeter or two. I wonder if the door did some type of self-correction to reseat the seal?"

They conferred for a minute or two after muting their mics, which I knew bothered Elin as much as me. "Come-on guys. Not fair."

Their shoulders lowered as if they knew they had to include us. "We don't see anything to indicate it was anything more than a glitch, but that doesn't mean it wasn't something. Just be careful up there, will you?"

"Will do. Thanks." Elin said before cutting the feed. She wiggled her shoulders as if trying to shake off her tension. "I still feel creepy."

"Should we have kept them online? Just in case."

She sighed and rolled her shoulders again. "And have all four of us staring at each other, waiting for something to happen? I don't think so."

"So, what would you rather do? It's almost time for you to start your sleep cycle."

"I'm far too tense. I won't sleep until we know what's out there or are certain nothing came inside."

"So, why don't I relax you?" We both hated using sex as a tool instead of a toy, but sleep was important. Especially with all the indications lately that we were in danger. It was necessary for us to be always at the top of our game.

She let out a pent-up breath and nodded, then sat down on her chair, which she'd vacated when the alarms sounded. She pressed the control to raise it to a comfortable height for me to thrust into her.

When the chair stopped moving, she draped her legs over the armrests, opening herself up to me. Despite the utilitarian reason for having sex, she was already wet. Her arousal glistened in the myriad of computer lights surrounding us.

I kissed her on the forehead before lining my hard cock up with her pussy. I stroked myself as I drew my cock through her folds, coating it with her juices before I plunged into her.

She gasped. "You always feel so good." She wiggled her ass to the edge of the cushion to give me better access. "Best relaxation technique out there."

I reached up to cup her breasts and tweaked her nipples with my fingers as we settled into our familiar rhythm. Sex with aliens was fun, but Elin and I had a special bond that made every interaction better than the last.

It didn't take long before she was writhing under me as I braced my arms against the back of her chair. As I leaned in close, the tips of her tits brushed against my chest as they bounced from the force of my cock plowing into her cunt.

Her inner muscles tightened around me, letting me know she was close. I brought my thumb to her nub and applied just enough pressure to detonate her orgasm. The clenching of her inner muscles was just what I needed to shoot my load deep into her pussy.

I bent down to kiss her, intending to rest for a few minutes before letting her get up to go to bed.

"Damian?!" she screamed a split second before I felt a quick slither up my legs and my arms were pulled out from under me.

My torso was suspended in midair. Arms strapped to my body, as I was still bent over Elin. My cock slid from inside her as I was pulled away and set on my feet. I was held captive by… snakes?

Big, angry-looking, black snakes with startling blue eyes.

They bound Elin too. Her legs and forearms were secured to her chair by a snake on each side, while a third slithered up between her breasts and raised its head above hers.

Its counterpart wrapped itself around my waist and stared me in the face. Its tail twitched back and forth, knocking against my now flaccid cock.

I recognized them from the database.

They were Nyoka, one of the 'shadow 'species who didn't ally with the Hooya and Rothrengal group. They were an unknown.

They fact they didn't announce their arrival, didn't bode well for us.

"They ssseem fragile." The one facing me said. Oddly enough, it didn't require the station to translate.

"They were dessscribed as soft." The one inspecting Elin swiveled its head toward me as it spoke. "They sssmell." it said as its forked tongue tasted the air around her. It moved over Elin's body, slithering around her breasts and then down her quivering abs as she took rapid, shallow breaths. Then its head disappeared below where I could see.

My view was blocked by the creature wrapped around me.

I didn't dare tilt my head to see where it had gone because the one around me was still staring at my face. It's brilliant blue orbs bulging out from the top of its flat head, which was cocked as if studying me. It's tongue flicking out too, as if tasting my reactions.

"They sssmell the same where they were joined." I felt its body move along my dick, making it jump in response. "Hmm."

It came into view again as he moved back up to face Elin. "What were you doing when we arrived? Were you mating?"

Elin glanced up at me before answering, fear evident in her eyes. "For pleasure." She told the Nyoka. "I was stressed, so we mated to relax me."

It paused, its tongue going double time as if searching for the truth in her words. "But you ssshared fluid. Isss that not how human procreation worksss?"

"It is, but I have been sterilized while I'm on this Outpost mission. I cannot reproduce here."

"The Othersss, ssseem to be fassscinated with humans. They have contestsss to visssit with you. We were not included."

"I'm sorry." I said, attempting to keep his attention from Elin. "We don't choose who we meet."

"We are aware." It craned its upper body to my height. "Whisssh is why we viewed you firssst. Insssstead of immediately desssstroying the new toys from Earth."

Elin let out a pained gasp.

I couldn't tell if it was from its words, or if one of them had hurt her.

"We like the way you sssounded before." It turned back to her. "Not frightened. How do I make you go back?"

Elin paused. I recognized her expression. She was reaching out empathically. Her expression cleared. "They feel betrayed but curious."

My tension eased. We may not die today after all.

"We have erogenous zones on our bodies. Places where we are more sensitive to pleasure. May I have one of my hands to demonstrate?" she asked.

The Nyoka who had coiled itself on her stomach nodded to the one on her arm. It freed her arm while keeping her leg imprisoned. "Our mouths are quite dexterous. We can taste and explore textures. We can't smell as well as you can.

At least, I'm assuming your physiology isn't much different than your counterparts on Earth. We can't taste the air."

"There are ssspecies like usss on Earth?"

"Yes, they are a vital part of our ecosystem." I added.

"We like being part." The head Nyoka said.

"Continue." Elin's captor slithered its head up her chest.

"These." She cupped the breast closest to her free hand. "If I have a child, I feed them from here. She tweaked her nipple."

Despite our situation, I felt a jolt of arousal.

The Nyoka reached forward and flicked its tongue across her puckered flesh, making her nipple and my dick both stiffen.

"Interesssting." It said as it wound his body between her tits.

"That feels good too." She told him. "The flesh is sensitive to the friction as you move over me."

"Sssentive? Ssso I can hurt you thisss way too?"

Elin looked at him with a sly expression on her face. "Some humans find a little pain pleasurable." She moved her hand slowly down her torso.

Its gaze was glued to her fingers as it swiveled its head to follow her motion.

The Nyoka who had coiled around me bent forward allowing me to get a better look at Elin.

"This is where we fertilize our eggs and give birth, but we are also designed for play. I'm assuming you watched how Damian fucked me."

"Yesss."

She spread the lips of her pussy open, exposing cum that was still sliding out of her slit.

My cock grew hard enough to alert the creature beside me. "He isss growing."

"It is pleasurable for me to watch her explore herself." I nodded to where her fingers were circling the tight bud of her clit. "And it heightens her enjoyment of her self-stimulation when she knows I'm aroused by the view."

The leader, coiled on Elin's stomach slid its head down for a closer view. Its tongue darted between her digits, and she gasped. "Again, please do that again." She moved her fingers, clearing a path for its tongue to taste her arousal.

It didn't hesitate. Its forked tongue slid along both sides of her clit, making her jump in response.

"Fuck yeah." Elin told him. "Just like that."

My captor's lower body was absently brushing against my erect cock as it rocked back and forth.

"Keep doing that." I told it. "Like Elin, the skin around my penis is also sensitive to touch and gives me much pleasure."

It wound down to observe how its body moved against mine. It wrapped itself around my cock and gave a test squeeze.

"Yesss." I said through my teeth. "Oh God, yeah. You feel like the inside of Elin's cunt."

"Inssside?" Her observer questioned.

"Yes." She panted. "Didn't you see Damian thrusting his cock into me? The friction as he moves in and out gives us both satisfaction."

The Nyoka on her belly raised its tail. For the first time, I could see what it looked like. It didn't taper off to a point. Instead, it had a thickly ridged blunt end, like a rattlesnake.

"Put that inside Elin, she'll love it."

Both of them watched as she slowly thrust her fingers into her hole.

The one on her stomach maneuvered its tail to ease its way between her outer lips and into her channel the way she showed them.

"Wow." She looked up at me. "Great idea, Damian. That feels fantastic."

"I'm going to squeeze my muscles around you as I would Damian's cock. Is that alright?"

Her captor nodded. "Yesss. I would like to feel that."

Its eyes, if possible, opened wider and the blue of its eyes glowed. "This isss pleasssurable."

The Nyoka who was wound around my waist, rose to meet my gaze. "Do you have such a place?"

"We both have other holes primarily used for discarding refuse from our bodies, but they are often used for fun, too."

"Ssshow me."

"I need a hand to balance so I don't fall when I bend over."

My captor hissed out an order and the Nyoka around my arm loosened its hold. The two who had been holding me prisoner now peered over my shoulder, watching, enthralled as Elin's Nyoka explored her snatch.

"My hole is between my ass cheeks. Elin has one too." Elin loved ass-play. She'd thank me later for planting the suggestion. I raised her leg and nodded to where her asshole winked. "There."

The guard adjusted its position around her newly extended leg, still holding her in place. Its tail crept toward her asshole. "She'll need lubrication. Make sure you are slippery before entering. Same with me. These holes require extra steps for maximum enjoyment."

The Nyoka holding Elin's leg moved its tail toward her clit. As it brushed against her hand, she stroked it with her fingers, making it slick. "Okay," she told it. "That should be good enough."

I reached down to help spread her ass cheeks and wipe a drop of pre-cum from my cock and worked it into her, then moved back to give its tail easier access.

Elin moaned as it entered her. With both of her holes filled and the one in charge, continuing to flick his tongue against her clit, her eyes closed. "Fuck me. That feels good."

"Me." My captor slid along my dick to give himself enough length to coil around my body to reach my ass.

"Wait, I need to lubricate you so it will feel better for both of us." It placed his tail in my hand, and I guided it to my cock's head, smearing pre-cum over its length.

"Okay, I'm going to bend forward to help you get in."

Seconds later, I felt it butting up against my entrance. I relaxed my muscles and felt every ridge as it slipped inside. I groaned as I stretched around its girth. So good.

"Amazing isn't it." Elin said as she lounged, every hole below her waist plugged by a Nyoka.

"Unbelievable." I agreed.

"Okay, to make this more enjoyable for us, and hopefully you too." Elin told them," You need to synchronize your movements. For me when one of you shoves in, the other comes out. This way you'll feel the friction not only against my skin but also against each other as you move. Keep flicking my clit with your tongue. When my muscles begin to involuntarily squeeze, you know I am

Amelia Dax

approaching the height of my pleasure. When I relax again, you'll know I've orgasmed."

"For me, it doesn't matter so much what order you go, just keep the rhythm. My muscles will also flex as I approach orgasm. When that happens, keep your face away from the tip of my cock, because my cum will spurt out."

"Thisss sssounds interesssting."

"I hope you like it as much as we will. You feel good already."

The Nyoka began to work. It took a few minutes for them to find their rhythm. Once they did, it was all I could do to grip the armrest under Elin's leg and hold on for dear life.

Holy fuck, that felt good. The rough texture of their blunt ridges sent sparks of arousal through my body. Their tails were flexible, able to bend back and forth in my chute, tripling the sensation as it moved in and out of me.

I raised my eyes to where Elin panted beside me. Her chorus of, "Oh, God. Oh, God. Oh, God." told me she was enjoying herself too, as both Nyoka fucking her were also tonguing her clit.

Mine must have thought that was a good idea, because he teased the slit on my cockhead with his forked tongue.

Elin screamed, "I'm cumming." at the same instant, my balls tightened.

"Watch out." I hollered, but it was too late.

The Nyoka licking my dick got a head full of cum. He didn't seem upset. He just kept squeezing my cock with his length until I was spent. Then the other ones, who didn't get to participate slipped from their positions to taste my jizz, and lick at Elin.

Elin was limp in the chair as I collapsed on top of her.

My legs couldn't hold me upright anymore.

She shifted to the side, to give me room to slide in beside her.

The Nyoka coiled together on top of us. Conversing in what I'll assume was their own language about what had transpired.

We could only hope that they decide not to kill us after all.

I was almost asleep by the time the leader spoke in English again. It was like a splash of cold water. I was instantly awake.

"Thank you for your generosssity." It said. "We underssssstand now why the Othersss are ssso enamoured with you."

"You showed fear, yet ssstill treated us as important. You did not disssressspect us." the one who'd buried himself in my asshole added.

"We recognize we are the weakest species. Our culture is new, and we are woefully unprepared for any sort of conflict." Elin told them. "Our hope is to learn all we can from others, and form strong alliances, until we can find our own strength."

"Then you will attack?" asked the head Nyoka.

"We value loyalty. We will always try to help those who've helped us." Elin said.

They conferred with each other again. "We are glad to have met you and are sssorry our arrival causssed you worry."

"Despite how it started, I think I can speak for Elin when I say we thoroughly enjoyed your visit."

"Definitely." Elin giggled. "Let us know if you can visit again. I'll research your anatomy and plan out activities that will bring you increased pleasure."

"We are honoured by this offer." All six aliens bowed their heads and closed their eyes, which only muted the intense blue of their gazes.

"It wasss worth facing possible punishment for sssircumventing the Allied One's sssystem to meet you."

"Can we help with that?" Elin asked. "I understand there is much discussion about who visits us next."

"We are outliers on the edge. Not included, not unincluded. Our action will make usss more unincluded."

"We'll see." Elin said. "We have friends in high places. We will try to prevent you from being punished. After all, you gave us a chance to prove ourselves, instead of harming us when you first arrived."

"Thank You." Then the leader turned, and the others followed it to the door. "We must leave you now. I believe our presssenssse has been detected by the Othersss."

"Take care of yourselves and thank you." I said as they slithered out of the room through the seam in the rubber seal where the doors met.

Seconds later, there was another door-breach alarm that lasted only seconds.

"Guys?" Faces appeared on our screens. "It's happening again. Only this time we can see something leaving the station."

"It's all right." Elin said with a smile. "Grab some lube before you play back the station's footage since we talked last."

"What?" All four members of our team on Earth crowded around their transmitting video camera. "That was only twenty minutes ago. How can lube-required shit happen in only twenty minutes?"

"Really?" I asked. "It felt like it was longer than that. More like an hour."

"Well, we didn't waste time with a lot of discussion between their arrival and our orgasms." Elin giggled. It was good to see her without the tension she'd had when our guests arrived. "We'll have an update on the…"

"Nyoka." I told her.

"The Nyoka soon. We have learned more about their culture and their place among the allied alien civilizations."

There was rapid fire typing in our cohort's room when one of them exclaimed, "Snakes? Aw hell no."

"Don't knock it til you try it." I said through my laughter at the horrified expressions on their faces. "Their jerk-off technique is spectacular."

"And that ridged tail." Elin feigned a swoon. "Unbelievable." She leaned toward our camera and winked. "They double barreled me. It was the absolute best."

All eyes on the other side ignored us and were glued to their monitor. I could hear Elin and my voices as they watched the playback. "Skip ahead to the last five or six minutes. Before the alarm went off again."

Elin's scream of. "Oh, God. Oh, God. Oh, God." Echoed through to us, making us smile all over again.

"Fuck. That's hot."

"Hey, can you do me a favour?" I asked them once the video finished, and I had their attention again. "Can you edit that down to eliminate the first part where they were threatening to kill us and leak the part where we teach them what to do to better enjoy the human body?"

"We don't leak video." The team lead said, while attempting to look innocent. The rest of the people in the room just snickered.

"I know you don't leak videos." I made finger quotes. "But seriously, that first bit isn't helpful to anyone. The sex part will help our population think even snakes can be sexy."

"I dunno man." One of the guys back on Earth said. "That's a hard sell. Yes, I had a hard on, but it was just from watching you get pounded, not because it was a snake doing it."

I sighed and glanced at Elin in exasperation.

"You know what I mean. Plus, I think it will help the cause and it will also save them some trouble with the Hooya and Rothrengal if they can see we enjoyed ourselves with them. They approached us because they were feeling left out. I don't want them punished as an example to others when we can use this encounter as a bridge instead."

"Good enough." The team lead said. "Who knows, maybe the other species who are on the fence about liking the humans will enjoy it."

"Yeah, just as long as they don't think we'd make a better snack than they previously thought."

"Licking is always better than chewing." Said the team supervisor, who'd just entered the room back on Earth. "What are we talking about?"

The crew replayed the last few minutes of the recording again. The newcomer's hand went to his crotch first to protectively cup his balls before his fingers started rubbing his bulge in sync with what was happening on the monitors. "Holy shit. Who knew that could be hot?"

"Well, guys, I'm tired." Elin said with a yawn. "I'm off to grab a shower and go to bed. Try not to wear out the video while I'm gone."

"Night Elin." The boys at home said in unison with me.

"Sleep well." I added.

Once she was gone, I asked the guys in a whisper. "Are we fucked completely, or do you think this little sex-capade helped ingrate us to the unallied aliens?"

The shrugs that answered me offered no comfort.

THE AGRESOIDS

DAMIAN

Elin and I were relaxing after our encounter with the Nyoka and wondering what kind of alien we'd encounter next.

Relaxing, of course, was an exaggeration considering we were in the middle of butt-fuck nowhere and didn't have close to adequate defenses. Three separate alien entities had easily breached our security systems.

We were sitting ducks in the middle of a very big and suddenly scary universe.

Our monitoring station crew interrupted the relative quiet of our station. "Hey guys, we're not sure what's happening out there, but the Hooya and Rothrengal ships are heading in your direction faster than I've ever seen them move. They're being followed by others in the Alliance."

"What did they say?"

"They aren't answering our query, or it's delayed because of stellar interference. We may not get their responses for hours."

Damn our primitive technology.

Elin looked grim. "Well, we knew we were in danger. I'm glad we don't have to wait any longer to see what's coming to get us."

"Yeah," I agreed. "The waiting was killing me."

"Let's just hope the killing part stays figurative."

Her words had just left her mouth when an oily-looking ooze covered the bottom half of her body. The shock on her face and the slimy feeling along my torso told me it was happening to me, too.

I tried to move, but my limbs were numb.

Between us, a shimmer appeared and then turned solid.

Two figures materialized. They towered over us so much they had to lower their massive heads to avoid hitting the ceiling. Their faces were terrifying. Large red eyes bulged from dull green skin that looked like scales. They reminded me of a drawing of a mythical dragon I saw as a child.

The resemblance didn't end there. They had elongated snouts and their sharp teeth extended past their lips. They had arms and legs but looked like they would move faster on all fours instead of standing erect. Behind them were thick tail-like protrusions, that ended with a stump that thumped against the floor in what I can only assume was irritation.

"Agresoids." Elin whispered.

We were in deep trouble.

Grunts emanated from their mouths and our ship's translator kicked in, making me wish it hadn't.

"They small."

"Not matter. Must take."

The bigger one, not that there was much of a difference, spoke again. "Dumb."

The smaller one shrugged. Their shoulders banged against the metal panels overhead. "Queen wants."

Elin and I looked from one to the other before our eyes met. We knew trouble didn't begin to describe the situation we were in. Even though we didn't have much protection on our station, we'd have nothing at all if we went to another ship. For the first time ever, our nakedness worked against us.

"Leave fast. Others close."

The slimy substance crept over Elin, covering her.

Then there was nothing. I was completely encased. Powerless to move. Sensations bombarded me. Dense weight as if I was being crushed, followed by a startling lightness as if my limbs were weightless, followed again by a heavy thump along my ass and shoulders. Another heavy weight bore down on me until the black ooze was pulled away, revealing my new surroundings.

It was not comforting.

I was lying on a platform in a clear compartment elevated almost a meter from the floor. I could see Elin in another one, a short distance away. The number of tubes and wires coming out of the top made me wonder if we'd survive the external atmosphere if we got free of our containers.

In front of us, stood several Agresoids. They looked bored as they stood facing the door past Elin's chamber. It opened and every being in the room straightened. This must be the queen.

She looked the same as the two that captured us, except she didn't have a tail that reached the floor. Hers instead was shorter and raised up. Almost perky in comparison.

Elin looked scared, but that's only because I knew her so well. To everyone else, she appeared intimidating. Head up, shoulders back and her fantastic tits front and center, nipples pointed, as if ready to do battle themselves.

This made my own little soldier rise to attention, which caught the eye of a few of the creatures standing beside my container. They nudged each other, nodding in my direction.

Interesting. That was, as long as they didn't think it looked like a toothpick, considering the size of their teeth. I snickered at the random thought, bringing everyone's attention to me.

Elin's eyes shot daggers in my direction. "Damian, what the fuck are you doing?" Then she jumped in surprise as her voice echoed throughout the greater chamber, followed immediately by a series of grunts, which had their entire delegation rumbling.

Were they laughing?

A sharp series of their language sounds heralded silence as the creature who'd entered looked at Elin with interest. "You are the leader?" The translation system said.

"We are equal." Elin's voice echoed over their translation system, only now, speaking in grunts.

"No leader?" the creature clarified.

"We have different specialties. We work as a team."

The creature seemed to ponder this for a moment.

"You lead your civilization?"

"We are ambassadors."

"You are important to your civilization."

"Yes. We make friends with other civilizations to protect ours."

"With pleasure, not war?" the queen questioned.

Elin grinned at me. We were back in familiar territory.

"Yes." I said, pulling her attention to me. "We prefer pleasure to war. Why destroy when you can build together?"

"Odd." The creature said. Then she pointed at my still hard cock. The greedy fucker was itching to get to the good stuff. "Weapon?"

"It's for pleasure." Elin said. "It makes us both feel good."

"Show me." She waved her clawed hand, and my container began to slide toward Elin's. Once they were flush, the joined side slid up, allowing us to move between the compartments.

I stepped into Elin's space. "Are you okay?" I asked.

"Yes." She whispered back. "You ready?"

"Always." I brought my lips close to her ear to avoid the translator picking up my words. "Should we take our time, give the Alliance a chance to get to us? I'm assuming that's why they were coming toward us so fast."

"Not a bad idea." Elin agreed as she reached up to kiss me.

"What are you doing?" The translator barked.

"Pleasure is good. It is best when we build up to the pinnacle and then feel its intensity."

A murmur went through the crowd. One of the smaller creatures spoke. "Research says this is how you procreate."

"Yes." Elin nodded. "Mating is enjoyable, and our species frequently does the mating act for pleasure alone."

A wave of shock went through the room. We heard a chorus of "Not for us." "It hurts" and questions like, "Can it hurt less?" and the response "Against the rules."

"Shit." I said to Elin. "No wonder they're cranky."

The translator crackled, echoing my words, and everyone stopped and looked at us. Some looked offended, and others looked curious.

"Pain makes us strong."

"On Earth, there is a similar ancient saying. What doesn't kill us makes us stronger, but our history shows that working together and overcoming obstacles through community and connection helps us to accomplish even more."

"We procreate artificially to avoid the pain of fertilization. Please show how you avoid this."

"Let the instruction begin." I said to Elin and then turned her so she was facing front. After a basic anatomy lesson, we started showing our audience how we touched ourselves and each other for arousal.

Elin's fingers circled her clit to showing how she self-lubricated while I stroked my cock. It didn't take long for pre-cum to leak out the end. Despite the danger we were in, I was still turned on. I moved toward Elin.

Elin moaned with pleasure as I circled her clit and massaged her breasts. Her channel was slick with need. I spread her legs a little more, bracing her against me so I could raise her leg to give the audience a better view. I swear, it made Elin get even wetter.

"There is a lot of wetness." the translator crackled.

"Because the friction when our bodies meet, requires a lot of lubrication. Our bodies secrete it throughout the mating process." Elin panted. "It eases the passage of his sexual organ into mine."

I released her leg and bent her over. We turned sidewise to our audience before I slide my cock into Elin. Every eye in the room bounced back and forth between her facial expressions and where our bodies joined.

The long tails of the males began thumping. Their chorus of grunts got faster as I increased my pace. Until they stopped being scary and were just another bunch of horny voyeurs.

Elin, always vocal, played it up even more. Keeping everyone focused on our actions.

I was having a hard time to keep from cumming. It was so hot watching Elin play the crowd of sexually frustrated creatures. At Elin's nod, I pulled out and grabbed my cock and jerked myself off for the last few strokes. The first shot of cum landed on Elin's back. The second on her ass, with the last few drops barely tipping out of the end of my softening cock.

I glanced out at our audience, and the thumping slowed to a stop. The murmurs in the room increased so quickly the translator couldn't keep up. Their surprise was unmistakable.

"Look at the floor." Elin said. "Isn't that the same ooze they used to capture us?"

The translator picked up her question.

"Yes." The queen spoke. "For generations it has been taken from our males. Part used to procreate, and the rest used for weaponry."

Another voice spoke. "This involuntary expulsion is unexpected and look, the colour has changed."

This was true. The black ooze looked greenish under the laboratory lights.

"It's a natural biological function." Elin told them. "Your physiology doesn't seem that different from ours."

"Where does your young emerge from?" I asked the Queen.

There was a ripple of shock through the room. "Silence." One of the more heavily clad creatures spoke up from near the door as they stepped forward. "Must respect."

The queen's hand flew up to stop him. "Stand down. I feel there is much to learn here."

He pointed a finger at her, "Make father angry." The offended creature warned.

"My father is dying and has placed me in charge. If you wish to question my authority, you may join him in imminent death."

Elin and I glanced at each other. Both of us saw an opportunity. We could create a new harmonious future for this civilization with this new regime about to take over.

"Before the process was automated, we birthed our offspring as eggs. The exit is just above the female's tail."

"How were the eggs inseminated?" Elin asked.

"The male's tail settles into the opening. The ooze transferred from male to female acted as both lubricant and fertilizer."

"The ooze has a numbing effect." I state. "Doesn't that help with the pain of intercourse?"

"It was forbidden. They told us it made us weak." The one who seemed in charge of the lab said. "The ooze as you call it, was collected for warfare, and fertilization left to the scientists."

"Were there any other factors that would prompt this decision?" Elin asked. I could see her brain spinning with ideas.

"There was a great famine. We set out to conquer new worlds because we couldn't support our growing population. During battles with the Hooya, Rothrengal and the other Alliance Worlds, our numbers grew too small and now we fight to survive."

Elin nodded. "I think I have solutions based on similar situations on Earth."

"Know nothing." The upstart from the doorway yelled before the queen's more loyal guards removed him from the room.

"Make sure he cannot communicate with my father or brothers. I will gather the information from the humans and make my own report." She turned back to us. "Continue."

"It sounds like you require a better form of birth control. Then you can have pleasurable mating without the risk of overpopulation. This will allow your world to support a healthy number without the need to attack other civilizations. Then you can join the Alliance and grow instead of fighting, which hinders your advancement and that of every species you encounter."

"Interesting." The queen said.

The translator started going nuts. "Issss here. They isssss here."

Elin disappeared in front of my eyes. I panicked until she reappeared with a big grin on her face. "Space Bugs." She said gleefully before disappearing again.

The door opened behind the queen, and an army of Nyoka slid into the room. "Ssssave him."

"Stop." I shouted at the factions about to do battle. "It's okay. We've got them sorted out."

The Ghost Gnome appeared beside me, along with the shimmering undulations of more space bugs waiting to take me away, as they did Elin. "We rescue you." He said, confused by my reluctance.

"It's okay. We can make peace."

The queen, cornered by a contingent of slithering snake-like creatures spoke. "I want to learn what the humans can teach us."

A Hooya appeared out of another mass of Space Bugs. They were almost unrecognizable in their battle garb. Their multiple heads chuckled as they took in the scene and realized what was happening. They turned to each other. "The humans have a unique ability to find connections. Don't they?" Then they spoke to the queen. "I'm glad you're receptive. Several ships are primed to attack if this incident cannot be resolved peacefully."

The translator sounded like it was broken, there were so many partial conversations happening at once.

Meanwhile the space bugs dissolved the container separating us from the rest of the large laboratory.

I put two fingers to my mouth and let out a shrill whistle. No translation needed.

Once I had everyone's attention, I spoke. "Thank you for coming to our aid." I did a half bow toward the Hooya and the Nyoka and then I patted the Gnome's little bald head beside me. Some of the Space Bugs draped over my shoulders in a show of support. They filled my senses with their pride.

"We have started a dialogue with the Agresoid Queen." I waved away the Nyoka still surrounding her. "Guys, let her be. She's wants to learn how we can help her civilization thrive without war. She is the new regime. Her father, the previous ruler, is dying and will not be a concern for much longer."

Just then the Rothrengal appeared beside a returning Elin. They both emerged from a cocoon of Space Bugs. Hopefully, their teleport experience was better than the one I'd just done courtesy of the black ooze.

To my surprise, the queen bowed her head when he appeared. "I'm sorry for our disrespect." She said as she rose. "I needed their help before my father caused another war."

The Rothrengal bowed his giant cock head in acknowledgement of her admission. The translator spoke. "I have been watching your struggles, my child. I am pleased you understood the importance of learning new ways to save your population. We feared it was your father and brother coming for the humans."

The queen rolled her bulging red eyes and smiled. At least, I assumed it was a smile. "Unfortunately, their information might have been accidentally inaccurate. They are heading toward your planet to intercept these famous humans."

I whispered to Elin, "That's one way to eliminate your competition for the throne." Apparently, I didn't speak softly enough. The translator echoed my words. Elin and I exchanged terrified looks. Had I just undone everything we'd accomplished?

The queen's eyes blinked three times, matching the beats of my now pounding heart. Then she bent over.

The entire room was eerily silent until huge guffaws of laughter were translated by the ship.

Elin jumped into my arms, and I held her close.

"This has been the most bizarre wake cycle I've ever experienced."

"Me too Babe. Me too."

The Rothrengal's wings patted me on the back while I could feel the Ghost Gnome slip around my body.

The horny little bastard wedged himself between my legs and from the way Elin's thighs tightened around me, I bet he was fucking her with his chin again.

Her gasp as he slid into her attracted everyone's attention to us.

Then it was pandemonium.

The Space Bugs dispersed over the crowd. They empathetically pulsated with Elin's arousal as they slid over the queen and her lab staff. The ambassador we nicknamed Maelstrom, (When the fuck did he arrive?) wandered through the crowd, taking dollops of the greenish-black ejaculation from the floor, and slapped it on the females. Using his cartoon-like hands to slide it into their holes above their tails.

Exclamations of "Ohh, it's warm," and "It tingles" rang out from the translator. As females demanded their male coworkers to continue where Maelstrom left off.

If I had to guess, I'd say the ooze, which now glowed bright green, was an aphrodisiac. Forcibly extracting from the males seemed to have altered its core properties, making it a weapon. Now it seemed to be a Spanish fly level lubricant.

In pairs, lab workers abandoned their stations. Their backs toward each other, the males pounded away at the female's entrance. The oozy lube squirting up with every thrust. No one looked in distress or pain.

Maelstrom was in the thick of it, helping to make sure everyone was getting some, and when there seemed to be too many females, he took the plunge himself. Bending over with his big nose he pumped into the nearest female. It must have been good, because I swear, I saw his eye stalks cross in ecstasy.

The queen was pushing away two of her bodyguards, whose tails were dripping with their ooze. "Stay away. I can't afford to mate now. Not when the throne is so close to being mine."

A battalion of Nyoka slid into place to protect the queen from her lust-driven kinsman. They leapt into action, wrapping themselves around the guard's tails, imitating the shape of the female's genitals. The guards stopped their pursuit of their queen. Their tails pumped hard as the Nyoka held on for dear life.

The queen vibrated with want. She was covered from head to toe in the dark green arousal fluid.

I passed Elin off to the Gnome who had started this whole orgy, to slip and slide my way over to the queen. "How can I help?"

"I need to be mated. But I can't." She wailed. "I need to stay unimpregnated until my position is official."

One look at her engorged mating entrance, I knew I'd be like a stone in a lake. She needed someone as wide as the males of her species'. "Hwan, I need your help." I called to my friend the Nevdu.

In seconds, he was beside me.

"I'm too small. Can you get big enough?"

He took a look at the queen's situation and nodded. "I would be honoured." He put his already engorged cock into her entrance and his testicles inflated quickly under his skin and started rolling against her inner walls.

The queen slapped her hands against the wall and screamed loud.

The translator echoed. "Fuck! That's good" in several different languages.

I turned around to survey the room to see the giant penis shaped Rothrengal sliding toward me in the ooze. His blow hole quivering in warning. I ducked just in time before his spunk hit the wall behind me. Blasting a hole into the next room where unsuspecting Agresoids seemed to be eating.

Thank the gods the Rothrengal wasn't pointed toward an exterior wall when he came.

The other Agresoids 'confusion was clear as they surveyed the scene through the hole in the wall. Their comrades were having unsanctioned wild sex with each other, joined by a mix of alien species including a huge penis shaped one, now laying limp on the floor, while a Nevdu fucked their queen.

Yeah, I'd be dumbfounded too.

The entity draped in cloth that normally assisted Maelstrom leaned against the wall. Their shroud quivering as they empathetically shared in the sexual melee.

A sated Elin and the Ghost Gnome stood beside the Hooya, enjoying the chaos, until the queen let forth a mighty roar as Hwan slumped over her tail, exhausted.

Then everyone started chattering at once. The queen being the last to experience an orgasm.

The translator wasn't able to keep up, so I whistled again. The shrill sound brought silence to the room, except for the squishing sounds beneath shuffling feet.

The floors and equipment were thickly coated with alien jizz.

Before I could say anything, a warning chime sounded, and a hologram appeared in front of the Hooya. Suspended in the hologram was a collection of ships, most of which I recognized as belonging to the Allied Aliens who had come for conjugal visits with us. I didn't recognize the new one approaching at an alarming rate except that it matched the one I presumed we were currently aboard.

"My brothers and father." The queen said angrily. "They've come to disrupt my mission of peace."

"We'll handle them." The Hooya said as they nodded at the shimmering Space Bugs. In seconds, they were engulfed and disappeared.

The hologram remained, and the room's occupants gathered around to view what was happening outside the ship.

As the king's vessel approached, the three tines of the Hooya ship drifted to the right and the Rothrengal's transport to the left.

The Space Bugs, visible only because of their great numbers, shielded the queen's ship as red warning lights flashed on her father's ship's hologram image.

A universal sign that they were readying their arms.

The light sped up, indicating the approaching onslaught as the ship turned away from the allies to aim at its twin.

"They want to kill me."

My heart broke for the queen. Her own family wanted to perpetuate war, even if it meant sacrificing a daughter. I put my arms around her waist, since she was still a meter taller than me. Her guards and co-workers bent at the knee and pledged their allegiance to her in what could be their final moments.

The red lights were now flashing so fast, they appeared solid. The room was silent as everyone held their breath.

Suddenly, there was a movement on the hologram. The space bugs lunged at the king's ship. They coated it with their bodies and while the red light kept steady, enormous gaps appeared in the ship's hull. The red light blinked one last time and faded while the ship disappeared, one Space Bug bite at a time.

Everyone's head bowed in respect for the now undisputed queen. The gains for her people were great, but her personal loss was greater.

After a few moments, she shuddered and then stood tall. "Thank you." She said to those of us who were still in attendance. "I came here with a half-formulated plan. I hoped to find a better way for our populace to live." She smiled at Elin and me. "You are truly the miracles you have been reputed to be. I thank you from the bottom of my heart." She bowed deeply before us.

Then she straightened and turned to Hwan. "One more for the road?"

Instantly, there was a cheer in multiple languages as we grabbed the nearest being and got busy.

EPILOGUE

5 YEARS LATER

Earth Outpost is better than ever. Elin and Damian are in charge of the Alien Outreach Program which has expanded to include other newly discovered worlds with relatively primitive defenses.

The Alliance of Planets has never been stronger There are other big bads out there, but none close enough to worry about.

Everyone is fucking like bunnies yet procreating responsibly. I'd tell you about it but I'm rather busy at the moment... the Hooya have just arrived for playtime.

BONUS CHRISTMAS EPILOGUE

DAMIAN

It was Christmas Eve, and Elin and I felt homesick. This was our first holiday season away from Earth and it was the first time we'd really felt far away from our families. Sure, we made video calls earlier, which made it better in some ways but also so much worse.

When our relatives hung up, we knew they'd continue getting ready for Santa while we were isolated, millions of kilometers away from everyone, watching for alien sneak attacks from species not allied with us.

To help lessen our homesickness, we decorated the station like we'd done as kids. The budget didn't stretch for frivolous things like decorations, so we made our own. Painting Santa and his sleigh on the window where we'd first seen the space bugs and watching silly Christmas cartoons from our childhood. Reruns that had been classics since the mid-1900s. Not only had they stood the test of centuries, but now, thanks to us, they were also officially popular off the planet Earth as well.

Both Elin and I loved shows from the twentieth century. We'd already watched the classic Rudolph the Red-Nosed Reindeer, giggled along with the Island of Misfit Toys and then we did a Grinch Who Stole Christmas marathon starting with the original cartoon and all versions right up to last year's virtual reenactment by the Holograms. To round off our first Christmas Eve in our home away from home, we'd saved our absolute favourite for last, the 1969 version of Frosty the Snowman.

It made us wonder about how, in the couple hundred years since it first showed on ancient televisions, nothing else was comparable. Even after Earth's religions merged when we finally realized how connected we all were. The entire concept of God morphed once we had a truer understanding of how vast the universe was and how small we were in comparison.

Once we stopped fighting over who had the better deity, Earth became a more peaceful place and we were able to do so much: eradicate hunger, control the climate and have more success in space exploration.

I mean, that's how we got an Earth Outpost to be stuck on this Christmas Eve.

We sat cuddled up in blankets from our beds. Elin in her computer chair and I in mine. We'd tried fucking away our loneliness earlier, but it just fell flat and made each of us feel worse.

The narrator for the cartoon was talking about the magic found in the first snow of the year, especially if it was on Christmas, when I suddenly felt sleepy.

I glanced over at Elin, and she was dozing off too. It wouldn't hurt anything if we both took a nap. The station's alert system would wake us up if anything important happened. Well, should wake us.

I was losing the fight with sleep as the voice on the cartoon sang, "There must have been some magic in that old silk hat they found."

The song echoed in my head, "Cause when they placed it on his head, he began to dance around."

As soon as the words came over the speakers, my eyes opened and the image of Frosty on the monitor winked. He grabbed hold of the sides of the screen and stuck his foot out over the lower edge and then stepped out onto the control board. As he ducked the rest of the way out of the monitor, he clasped his hat to its head and then jumped to the floor in front of me.

I heard Elin gasp beside me. I glanced over to see her fully awake now with a huge grin on her face.

"Hey, Damian. I'm Frosty. It's a pleasure to meet you." Then he turned to Elin and bowed low. "It's even more of a pleasure to meet you, Elin. I've been looking forward to making your acquaintance for a long time."

She giggled. "I never dreamed I'd meet you in person." She said. "You've always been one of my favourite parts of Christmas."

"Well, my dear. That's lovely of you to say. Hopefully, I can make your Christmas even better. Santa tells me you've been a very, very naughty girl this year, in all the best ways."

She laughed again and tossed her blanket to the side, spreading her legs wide open for him. "I thought I was being good all year. Very good, in fact."

Frosty's corn-cob pipe bobbed as he swallowed and then his cartoonish smile got even bigger. He glanced back at me and winked. "That's also what I heard."

He reached out and stroked Elin's pussy. Rubbing his thumb up and down the crease between her legs, using his other hand to spread her lips open wide so he could play with her clit.

"Fuck, Frosty. You're cold." She said, as gooseflesh erupted on her thighs and stomach. "Don't stop." she cried out when he hesitated. "It feels fantastic."

"Well, in that case, have you ever been fucked by a popsicle?"

She winked at him. "Once, but it was summer, and it melted way too fast."

"I'm a lot of things, but fast isn't one of them." He said as he kept circling her sensitive clit with his thumb and then entered her slick channel with his thick, snowy fingers.

"Holy Fuck, that feels good." She opened her legs wider, giving him as much room as she could. "You're so cold, but so hot at the same time."

I'd already tossed my blanket aside and angled myself to watch them instead of the monitor where the cartoon was still playing. My fingers closed around my cock, and I gave it long slow strokes in time with Frosty's fingers as they fucked Elin.

"Thank God, they drew you with all five fingers." She panted. I recognized the signs. She was close to cumming all over his hand.

Frosty sped up his movements, the friction making him melt just a bit onto the floor as he leaned forward, spit out his corncob pipe and latched on to one of her nipples. The cold on her breasts was the final touch that brought her to a resounding orgasm.

Gooseflesh peppered her torso as she shattered under him.

"That was unreal." She said as she leaned back against her chair.

"I can do better." He said as he reached up to his carrot nose and pulled it right off his face.

"Wait, doesn't the song say you're supposed to have a button nose?" She asked?

Frosty just rolled his eyes and looked conspiratorially over at me. "Have you ever tried to fuck somebody with a button?"

I shook my head. "Nope."

With that he turned the carrot around and stuck the thin pointy end into his lower stomach, leaving the thick, stem end sticking up proudly from between his legs. Then he swiped snow from his stomach, leaving ridged abs, and took the two handfuls of snow and jammed them under his carrot penis.

I laughed in spite of myself. "Snowballs."

"Aren't you glad I upgraded to a carrot?" he asked Elin.

In a split second, she had his carrot in one hand and snowballs in the other. "Let's rock around your Christmas carrot." She reached up and pulled him down on top of her.

Frosty wasted no time. He nuzzled her neck and then gently pushed her back. Her nipples were hard as rocks from the chill coming from him.

She arched her back, and they rubbed their bodies together before he leaned back just enough to position his carrot. He slid the blunt end of his veggie-prick between her pussy lips. Gathering moisture from her recent orgasm to ensure he was well lubricated before easing the long length of his root vegetable into her snatch.

"Damian!" She looked over at me. "If I'm dreaming, do not pinch me to wake me up. I'm getting fucked by Frosty."

"If you're dreaming, so am I and I'm enjoying the show too much to want to wake up."

"If you think this is great, wait until your turn." Frosty's smile held so much promise I almost came on the spot.

He shifted his attention back to Elin. The muscles in his newly carved out abs flexing with every thrust. His snowballs hitting against her ass with a slushy slap. His hands molded to her breasts, icy fingers pinching her nipples until they were rigid and nearly blue with the cold.

I was about to be concerned about hypothermia when she screamed. "Don't stop." She wrapped her legs around his waist and pushed her hips up to grind against him every time their bodies smashed together until her legs tightened, and she hollered again. "Fuuuuck."

It took Frosty three more strokes in her tight cunt before he pulled out, his slushy cum decorating her stomach. "Christmas snow is potent. Don't want any little snow angels running around next year." He said with a laugh.

He tenderly took Elin's blanket and used a corner to wipe his cum from her body. Then he wrapped the rest of it around her and kissed her forehead. "Don't want you to catch a cold."

Then he turned to me. "You've been a very naughty boy this year, Damian. Do you want to top or bottom?"

His question took me off guard. I hesitated. I'd had all sorts of inappropriate thoughts of Santa cumming but never considered sex with a snowman.

Before I could answer. Frosty gave a laugh. "Just joking my boy, we'll do both." He stepped between my legs and lifted them up over his shoulder, pulling me down the seat cushion until my ass was hanging over the edge.

Elin, ever on the ball, reached over and reclined the back of my chair to make me more comfortable.

Frosty's body was cold where it touched me, but it did nothing to shrink my raging hard-on. With my legs balanced, he spread apart my ass cheeks and slid his fingers along my crack.

Instantly, my muscles relaxed. They were as eager to have him inside as I was. I was about to get fucked by Frosty. "Merry fucking Christmas to me."

Apparently, a little of that Christmas snow magic rubbed off on the carrot. It wasn't as hard as I expected it to be. It felt like a silicone toy as it slid past my sphincter, filling me like a stocking from Santa. His snowballs slapped against my ass as he drove as far as he could into me. The cold of their touch against my heat amplified every sensation.

It was intense. The hot and cold set my ass on fire as he stroked every nerve ending inside my chute, sending jolts of electricity through my body until I was sure I'd cum like a laser cannon. He leaned forward and grabbed my dick in his hand. There was no shrinkage. In fact, I think I grew three sizes that way.

He stilled and let me push back over his carrot dick and then rise, pushing myself up, using his shoulders as leverage to plunge into his grip, back and forth until I knew he should be melting into a puddle from how hot it was.

It took only a few more thrusts, and I was a goner. Spurts of cum exploded out of my dick, arching in the air like a candy cane.

A few more thrusts and Frosty pulled out and instead of dodging his cum as I'd done mine, I raised myself up on my elbows, trying to catch it as it flew through the air.

Peppermint. He fuckin' tasted like peppermint.

Elin spooned up a glob where it landed on my chest. She let it sit on her tongue for a moment before exclaiming. "I knew it. Frosty cum is candy cane flavoured."

Frosty laughed and turned around, sticking the big, round snowball of his ass in the air.

"One more hole to go." He said with a wink.

Elin and I both cocked our heads as we searched for an opening in his pristine, snow-covered butt.

"But there's no hole?" Elin's statement came out as a question.

"Oh, pardon me." He stood up and pulled his carrot dick out of his front and handed it to me. "You can do the honours. Put it wherever you want."

I held the carrot like a dagger. But then I realized the resulting hole wouldn't give me a good angle to fuck him, so I lined it up with my already hard again dick and made an indent.

"Ohhh, that tickles." Frosty said with a giggle and a wiggle of his big snowball ass.

"Ready?" I asked him as I added pressure to the carrot.

"Yes, please." He leaned forward to brace himself on the ledge in front of the computer controls.

With a slow steady pressure and a little swivel motion, I bored Frosty a brand-new asshole.

"Happy Birthday." He shouted with glee, then glanced back at me over his shoulder. His eyes of coal looked hooded with desire. "Now, fuck me with your fucking thing, fucker."

Frosty was a dirty talker, which made me even harder for him.

I tossed the carrot over my shoulder and put the head of my cock against his freshly made hole. It drew me in and swallowed me whole until my balls were snuggled against him.

He flexed his inner muscles around me, and I almost made a snow cone on the spot.

I pulled out and shoved myself back into him. Despite the heat generated between us, he stayed snug against my skin with every stroke. It didn't take long for me to increase the pace and pummel into him with all I had.

His crystalline cold against my rigid dick made every nerve stand at attention. I was a thrusting machine, thumping into him hard with every plunge into his cool depths.

"I'm cumming." I cried out an instant before I let loose in his asshole.

I banged him until I was spent, and then staggered back to my chair before I collapsed.

Frosty seemed to be just as affected. It took him several minutes before he stood upright and turned around.

Immediately, I was filled with remorse. "I'm so sorry, I never thought…"

The front of his snowy tummy looked like an exit wound. My hot cum had shot through him, melting part of his middle.

He waved away my concern. "Occupational hazard." He said as he reached down and took off his balls and packed them into his stomach to plug the holes before smoothing his hands over the surface. When he removed his hands, you'd never have known I got carried away. "See." He said. "Good as new."

He bent over and picked up the corn-cob pipe he'd dropped earlier when he sucked on Elin's nipples. "I hate to love you and leave you, but there are a lot of naughty boys and girls like yourselves who I have to visit tonight." He winked again and jumped up onto the console and put his leg over the bottom edge of the monitor, where the cartoon had almost finished. He held onto his hat as he ducked back into the Christmas scene on the screen. Seconds later, he turned back into the 2-D drawing and hopped into Santa's sleigh.

Thumpity thump thump, thumpity thump thump, look at Frosty go…

My eyes flew open, and I stared open mouthed at the screen. "Was that real?" I asked myself out loud as Elin woke up beside me.

"I just had the craziest dream." Her brow puckered as if trying to solve a puzzle. "It was a dream, right?"

We looked at each other and they looked at the monitor. Frosty was in Santa's sleigh and they took off from the group of children, flew in front of the moon and then swept in a circled back to in front of the camera. Frosty winked and blew us a kiss. "I'll be back again someday."

"No fucking way." I muttered. "He always says he'll be back on Christmas Day in this version."

"Did he fuck us in your dream too?" she asked.

"Yeah. And then I fucked him and forgot to pull out."

"And blasted a hole right through him."

We looked at each other.

"That can't be possible." Then I shivered. "But I'm as cold as fuck now."

"Me too." She said as she gathered her blanket around. "Want some hot chocolate?"

"Sure."

She stood up and immediately screamed and jumped back into her chair. Feet on her chair and arms wrapped around her legs. "There's cold water on the floor." This time, she gingerly stepped around the puddle. "It's not possible." She muttered as she went over to the counter to make our beverages.

I looked under my chair to see water pooled there, too. Right where Frosty had been standing when he was plowing into me. I glanced at the console ahead of me and saw watery globs of my cum starting to dry on the ledge. "Can't be." I muttered. "Impossible."

Then I froze as a memory burst into my consciousness. I was almost afraid to turn around, but I did anyway.

Sure enough, on the floor where I threw it was Frosty's upgraded carrot nose. "Uh, Elin…" I pointed to the carrot as she turned around. "Look."

She fell back against the counter. "It was real." Then she started giggling. "We fucked Frosty."

The credits were rolling at the end of the cartoon, and I reached up with the edge of my blanket to wipe a clump of snow off the bottom of the monitor.

Elin watched as I tasted it. "It tastes like me."

"Too bad you don't taste like peppermint like Frosty."

I made a face. Even I could admit my semen didn't have the greatest flavour. "This is true."

"I wonder if they got it on video, or if it was Christmas Magic just for us."

"No one would believe us." I said as I set the system to display the last twenty minutes. "I was disappointed, but not surprised, to see it showed Elin and me napping for the whole time. Although just before we woke up, there was a blur at the bottom of the screen and the carrot appeared out of nowhere, bounced twice on the floor before stopping where it still sat on the floor.

Elin stepped around the puddles and handed me a mug of hot chocolate. "Merry Christmas." She said as she raised her cup for a toast.

"Merry Christmas." I replied, clinking our cups together.

Then we both raised our mugs to the monitor. "Merry Christmas, Frosty." We said together.

AFTERWORD

I hope you enjoyed this little romp through the stars.

Please leave a review on Amazon, Goodreads, or wherever you bought this book. Reviews matter more than you know.

Stay Sexy,
Amelia

AUTHOR BIO

Forgettable by day and incredible at night, Amelia Dax writes what we all hope first contact is really like. Taking inspiration from the worlds around us she crafts stories of lust and satisfaction. She truly believes we should make love, not war.

WATCH FOR HER NEXT NOVELLA

'HORNI-CULTURE'.

A collection of short stories that tell the tale of four sets of survivors.

After a rapid-fire series of worldwide illnesses ravage the earth, where the last one left most of the remaining population resembling zombies, our few survivors are grateful for a harsh winter that seemed to release them from the threat of the undead.

But the following spring, they discover strange plants that resemble body parts growing from the earth.

Coming in September 2024, have your hand and/or batteries ready to read about the Penis Plant, Pussy Willow, Helping Hands and Playing Footies.